Note to Readers

While the Schmidt family and their friends are fictional, the events they find themselves in are real. World War I, or the Great War as it was called then, was one of the bloodiest wars in history. Many young men died fighting for freedom.

Life was difficult at home as well. Families went without flour, meat, and gasoline so that there would be more supplies for the army. Hundreds of thousands of peach pits were collected to be used in gas masks for the soldiers. The poison gases that were used against the soldiers caused such horrible deaths and injuries that, after the war, nations agreed to never use poison gas in war again.

While the Mennonites Carl meets are fictional, the persecution they faced was experienced by Mennonite communities throughout the country. Many Americans whose sons were dying on the battlefields in France found it hard to be tolerant of people whose religious beliefs did not allow them to fight in the army.

☆ The ☆
GREAT
WAR

Norma Jean Lutz

BARBOUR
PUBLISHING, INC.
Uhrichsville, Ohio

Especially for you, Kerry. With all my love!

Published by Barbour Publishing, Inc.
P.O. Box 719
Uhrichsville, Ohio 44683
http://www.barbourbooks.com

 Member of the
Evangelical Christian
Publishers Association

Printed in the United States of America.

Cover illustration by Peter Pagano.
Inside illustrations by Adam Wallenta.

CHAPTER 1

Victory Garden

The scraping of the garden hoe grated in Carl's ears as he swung and chopped, swung and chopped to eliminate the pesky weeds that tried to invade the rows of snap beans. Sweat trickled down his face and back. He itched so badly he wanted to lie down and roll in the grass like a horse.

Carl straightened for a moment and let his arms and back rest. A dull throbbing pumped through his arms and shoulders. The hot June sun was baking his little garden faster than he could keep it watered, and the hoeing was backbreaking work.

Pulling off his straw hat, he swiped at his face with his

handkerchief, which was smeared with dirt. When Mama first suggested he wear a straw hat, Carl had cringed. How silly looking! But Uncle Erik, who along with his wife, Aunt Esther, had tended an older relative's farm for nearly four years, agreed with Mama. "Take it from me. There's nothing like a straw hat to shade the face and still allow air to circulate."

Since Uncle Erik said it, and since Carl admired his newspaper-reporter uncle, then it must be so. And it was.

Tending a vegetable garden had caused Carl to discover muscles he never knew he had. The pain had lessened, but two months ago when he first tilled up their hard-packed backyard for a "victory" garden, Mama had to rub him down with foul-smelling liniment every night. In all his fourteen years, he'd never known so many achy places. How did old Mrs. Bierschwale next door do it?

He looked over the fence at their neighbor's thriving garden. Tomato plants already stood a foot tall, and dark green vines—probably melons and cucumbers—swirled around here and there. In spite of his hours and hours of hard work, Carl's garden paled in comparison.

"*Guten Morgen*, Carlton," came the familiar greeting from across the slatted fence. Mrs. Bierschwale had appeared from nowhere, calling him, as she did all the Schmidt children, by his full name. Her dark cotton dress hung shapelessly on her thin bent frame, and her tattered and frayed straw hat was perched precariously atop her silvery hair.

"Good morning to you, Mrs. Bierschwale."

"Another load of rotted manure you will be needing, looks like."

Carl rubbed at his back. "Another load?"

The way she studied his garden irritated Carl. After war

had been declared in April and after President Wilson had urged every American family to grow a victory garden, Carl had appreciated all the advice from old Mrs. Bierschwale—especially pointers about making a compost pile in the corner where he chopped up all the weeds and dumped in all the kitchen scraps to rot into rich loam to feed his plants.

But now he resented her remarks, and he wasn't sure just why. He'd lost count of the wheelbarrow-loads of rotted manure he'd brought from the local livery and shoveled onto his little garden plot. Now she said it needed more.

"And," Mrs. Bierschwale added, "breaking up ground in autumn iss much better. If not autumn, surely by March thaw time."

"I know, Mrs. Bierschwale," Carl replied, trying his best to keep the irritation out of his voice.

She'd told him that at least a hundred times. Papa said she tended to forget what she'd said, so he tried to be patient.

"Last fall," he reminded her, as he had so many times before, "I didn't know we'd be at war, nor that I'd be under presidential orders to grow a victory garden." Nor did he know he would be the only available person in the Schmidt family to do most of the work. But he didn't say that part out loud.

"Vat does Vilson know?" she said with a wave of her gnarled old hand. "Iss gute to grow der garden, war or no."

Carl supposed she was right. His younger sister, Edith, whom they all called Edie, had taken his early lettuce and made tasty helpings of wilted lettuce cooked in bacon grease with onions chopped over it. And the family had eaten handfuls of the radishes and baby carrots and raved about them. Papa was especially fond of the early onions.

Even Carl enjoyed the vegetables and felt proud to have produced them.

Still, he longed to be back in the shed that housed his darkroom and to once again spend hours on his photography projects. He leaned on the hoe a moment and gazed at the building that he and his friend Truman Vaught had fixed up together.

First Truman had left them to travel to France and serve with the American Field Ambulance. Then when the United States declared war in April, Truman had rushed home to join the army. He was now a uniformed doughboy in training at Ft. Sheridan, Illinois. And Carl was so busy growing a garden and throwing his paper route each day, there was precious little time for photography. Besides that, without Truman around, much of the fun had gone out of his photography work.

"Ach, Carlton Schmidt," came Mrs. Bierschwale's voice again. "Lean on der hoe and der veeds vill grow right over top of you."

She chuckled softly at her own joke.

Carl replaced his hat, raised the hoe, and went back to chopping, breaking up the clods and cutting out the weeds. Ever since he'd mulched his tomatoes with straw, just as Mrs. Bierschwale had told him, they were doing much better. "Der feet to be cool, they like," she told him in her broken English.

Sometimes he wished she didn't have such a strong German accent. Ever since the outbreak of war in Europe three years earlier, German Americans had been looked upon with suspicion and mistrust. They'd been accused and suspected of everything from spying to sabotage. It was bad enough to have a German name like Schmidt, let alone have a strong accent such as Mrs. Bierschwale and her husband, Bruno, had.

She came over to the fence again. "Iss the day for to sign

men up for war," she said. "My Bruno and me, we hear the factory whistles blow. Church bells ring. Like a celebration it sounds." She clucked her tongue. "Such nonsense. Americans, they will not stand for it, nein?"

Carl gave a shrug. "I don't know, Mrs. Bierschwale," he said and went on hoeing. Carl knew that this Tuesday, June 5, 1917, all men between the ages of twenty-one and thirty were to register for the draft at their local polling places. He'd read in the paper just that morning that the factory whistles were to sound as a reminder of the event.

Talk had it—both in rumor and in the papers—that people would not abide with the government calling up men to fight in the war. Some railed against the idea, saying it was unconstitutional. There was speculation that protesters would riot in the streets. Papa told the rest of the family that men had not been forced to take up arms and fight since the Civil War. That was a very long time ago—more than fifty years.

"Iss like old country where men are forced into war," Mrs. Bierschwale said.

Carl finished one row of beans and turned to start up the second row. He didn't know how the draft would be received, nor if that was like the "old country" or not. But how else were they to help win the war over there in Europe if they didn't call up men to serve? When he kept hoeing and didn't answer, Mrs. Bierschwale went back to work among her lush vegetable plants.

Just then the back door slammed and Edie stepped out on the back stoop. Her cat, Frosty, bounded out and came to the edge of the garden, eyeing it suspiciously.

"I'm leaving to take the trolley to go to Aunt Frances's house," Edie said. "Is there something you need before I go?"

Carl grinned. "Will you finish the hoeing?"

Edie hated getting dirty and had barely set foot in the garden since he first started spading it up. Mama sided with Edie, saying since she did all the cooking and cleaning while Mama, Papa, Tim, and Lydia were all at work, Edie could be excused from gardening. Carl's younger sister also worked as a mother's helper for Aunt Frances and Aunt Esther, which kept her busy three afternoons a week.

"Anything other than that?" Edie said, ignoring his attempt to tease. She came after Frosty and took him up in her arms, snuggling him close.

"A drink of water would be appreciated," Carl told her.

A short while later, Edie brought him a tall glass of water. On top floated a clear piece of ice, which she'd chipped from the block in the icebox. Mama didn't like them to chip the ice block. The block lasted much longer if it were left alone. He knew Edie had done it as a special favor for him. The ice clinking against the glass had a nice cool sound to it. He took a long satisfying drink, then wiped his mouth with his sleeve.

"It's looking very nice," she commented, nodding her head toward his garden.

"It's not much compared to the one next door," he replied lowering his voice so Mrs. Bierschwale couldn't hear.

"Don't forget she's had about a twenty-year head start," Edie said with a smile. "That is, if we're considering her present garden. Maybe *fifty* years or more, considering other gardens she's had in past years."

"All right," Carl said, handing his sister the empty glass. "Your point has been taken." He looked back over his rows of beans, which were beginning to actually have real beans growing on the vines. "Maybe it's not such a bad garden after all."

Mama had told him when the beans were ready, she and

Edie and Lydia would preserve them in canning jars and they could eat them next winter.

"It's as fine a victory garden as any in the city of Minneapolis," Edie assured him.

"Thank you," Carl said, knowing full well that his twelve-year-old sister had seen only a few of the gardens in the city.

As Edie started back into the house, he said, "Tell Larry I'll take him to the dump to gather scrap iron on Saturday. It's part of his Boy Scout project."

Larry was the eldest of Aunt Frances and Uncle Richard's three children, but at age nine, he was still in knee pants. Sometimes he seemed more like Carl's younger brother than his cousin.

"I'll tell him," she answered. And she was gone.

The place seemed strangely quiet after Edie left. Usually Carl didn't mind being alone, but ever since Truman went away, Carl wrestled with a strange loneliness he couldn't quite explain. Even though Papa and Carl's older brother Timothy were kind and supportive of all that he did, Carl felt closer to Truman than anyone else.

Truman had worked with him in the darkroom, taught him about lighting, and showed him new techniques to use with his camera. Every time Carl thought about Truman fighting in the war, his eyes burned with tears. He stopped and pulled his dirty handkerchief out again and pressed hard against his eyes. Maybe it was just the salty sweat that made them burn.

At that moment the postman's whistle sounded from the front of the house. Carl leaned the hoe against the back stoop, pocketed his handkerchief, and went around the side of the house.

"Mornin', Carl," Mr. McCracken called out. Even the postman was breaking a sweat on this warm day. "It appears you've been digging in that victory garden of yours," he said, eyeing Carl's dirt-caked trousers.

"Yes, sir." Carl wiped his sweaty hands on his pants legs and looked hopefully at the bulging leather bag slung over the postman's shoulder. Every day they watched and waited for letters from Truman. "Anything for us in there?"

"If you mean letters from an army camp in Illinois, the answer is yes." He dug around in the bag for a moment, then pulled out a grocery flyer advertisement, a bill from the power and light company, and finally a letter!

Carl could tell at a glance that it was from Truman. His heart skipped a beat. He reached out to take the mail, but Mr. McCracken said, "Just a minute, that's not all." Pulling out still two more letters, he said, "I don't see how those boys have that much time on their hands to be able to write so many letters."

Carl looked at the three envelopes. One was to the family, and one was to Lydia. He'd expected that. After all, his older sister often received personal letters from Truman. Carl had caught the two of them kissing on the back stoop before Truman left to report to training camp. Of course, he'd never tell Mama. For that matter, Lydia probably didn't know she'd been seen. Sometimes Carl felt a little jealous that Truman would pay so much attention to Lydia. Especially after he and Truman had become such close friends.

Then he looked at the third letter. It was addressed to Carlton Schmidt! Truman had written a letter just to him. Quickly, Carl bade Mr. McCracken good-bye, took the other mail inside to the kitchen table, then hurried out to his darkroom hideaway to read his letter.

CHAPTER 2

Jillian Oliver

As he pushed open the door to his darkroom, Carl was met with the old familiar aromas of chemicals used to develop photos. Even that aroma made him miss Truman. They'd hung a heavy drape to divide the shed, creating the darkroom at one end. At the other end was a cabinet where photos were stored, a set of shelves loaded with Carl's collection of books, and an old cast-off chair where he could sit and read.

He sat down now, propping the chair back against the wall, and tore open the letter. It started with the words *Greetings to my pal, Carl.* Carl could almost hear Truman talking. He glanced over at the photos pinned up on the wall. Several were of him and Truman. One was a close shot

13

of Truman's handsome angular face, laughing eyes, and dark hair combed straight back. He never had a hair out of place. That photo was taken when Truman was teaching Carl about what he called "portrait" photography.

"People's faces can be a source of fascination," Truman had said. "Through photography, we can capture the essence of a person."

Carl had seen very few photographs of just a person's face. It took someone like Truman to think of such a thing.

Carl sighed and turned to Truman's letter. It described rising before dawn to the sounds of the bugler playing "Reveille," eating breakfasts of thick, tasteless oatmeal, making long, tiring marches with a heavy pack on his back, crawling through grueling obstacle courses, and practicing strenuous drills with bayonets fixed on their guns.

We run as hard as we can at those hanging sandbags and then ram our bayonets right into them. Everything we do here is getting us ready for the battlefield. Even though it's very demanding, I'm ready to give my all for the cause of freedom in our world.

Ramming a bayonet into a sandbag—practice that would one day prepare them for actually killing another person who was called the enemy. Carl heaved a big sigh and read on.

I've heard the news that President Wilson has decided to create a draft system for bringing in new troops. I know that must be done. But I'm praying the president will also make arrangements for those whose personal beliefs do not allow them to take up arms. You may know I'm thinking specifically of the Mennonites. Because they are pacifists and because they are German Americans, they may have a rough time of it.

I knew many good, kind Mennonite families when Ma and I lived over in New Ulm, before we moved to Minneapolis. I pray God the government will not be cruel enough to force those godly gentle people to join in the fray. There are more than enough men who are willing to fight without forcing those who cannot and will not do so because of their beliefs.

Carl had never thought about such things before. But of course Truman would. Truman was so unlike any person Carl had ever known. So strong in his own principles and yet giving others the space to have their own ideas as well.

When Lydia came home from her job at Woolworth's that evening, she grabbed her letter and ran upstairs to read it in private. Mama and Papa were understanding. Although Lydia didn't come down to supper until after they'd already begun to eat, no one said a thing.

When she pulled out her chair and sat down, Papa was sharing news he'd heard at the mill that day. Papa worked as a foreman at the Northwest Consolidated Flour Mill. He also served as the president of the mill workers union, a position which had caused no small disruption in their lives. That was because so many people hated the labor unions.

"There's talk of a plan," Papa told the family, "to cut back on flour usage in our homes here in the States so we can ship more flour to the Allies. We heard that officials in Washington, D.C., will be putting the plan into action as soon as possible."

Edie, who did a good deal of the cooking, was silent for a moment and then asked, "Cut back using flour? How?"

"Perhaps we'll be asked to use substitutes," Mama suggested. "Or not use as much."

"But we use flour in nearly everything—bread, biscuits, muffins, cakes, pie dough, *Spätzle* noodles." Edie counted on her fingers. "I even use flour to thicken gravy. I don't see how we could cut back."

"Where there's a will, there's a way," Tim quoted. "I'm sure we can do most anything if it means helping the war effort."

Papa nodded. "We, more than others, must make every effort to be in the forefront of as many of the war efforts as possible."

Carl knew what Papa meant. As German Americans, they would have to be more diligent than others to show their patriotism.

"I suppose that means liberty bonds as well," Mama put in.

"Even the liberty bonds," Papa said. "We will purchase them as often as we are requested to do so."

The concern in Mama's eyes couldn't be disguised. Even with all of them working and scraping, it took every penny to make ends meet. Where the money would come from to purchase the bonds, no one knew. Gigantic bond rallies were already being staged around the country, and American citizens were compelled to purchase bonds to fund the war machine that was gearing up.

Carl had seen a poster in the window of the post office downtown that said: *Beat back the HUN with liberty bonds.*

Above the caption was an illustration of an evil man with a spiked helmet and a bayonet dripping blood. *Hun* was the word everyone used to describe the hated Germans. It was also the name of the people who had invaded that area of Europe hundreds of years ago. Just the word made Carl shudder, let alone the picture.

When Mama, Lydia, and Edie had the dishes washed and put away, the family gathered in the parlor to read aloud Truman's letter to the whole family. "To the Schmidt family," the salutation read. In the first part of the letter he repeated some of the things that were in Carl's letter about the rigors of training. Then he wrote:

> *Our commanding officer is from West Point and is every inch a soldier. To a man, we all respect him. He's firm yet fair with all his men. I'm amazed at how quickly our government has put this training camp together. You see nothing but tents for miles—rather like a small city. New wooden barracks are being built even as I write this letter.*
>
> *On the outside of camp are volunteers from the Red Cross and the Y.M.C.A. They feed us full of doughnuts, homemade pies, and mugs of hot coffee. They also hold church services for us every Sunday morning.*
>
> *My outfit has won awards for being top-notch in every area of our training. We've been told we'll be one of the first ones to ship out. It looks like I'll be back in France by the Fourth of July. How fitting! Don't worry, though. I'll let you know as soon as we have word!*

"He sounds so excited," Edie said when the letter was finished. "How can anyone be excited about going to war?"

"It's because he's doing what he believes to be right," Lydia said.

"I clean the bathroom because it's right," Edie countered, "but I sure don't get excited about it."

Everyone laughed, and their mood lightened. To think of Truman leaving for the battlefront before the Fourth was sobering indeed.

Carl slipped away the next afternoon, riding his bicycle downtown to the Bijou Theater to see a flicker. Of all the shows that came to town, the Westerns starring William S. Hart were his favorite. When he was younger, he'd covered the walls of his bedroom with travel posters proclaiming the attractions of the Wild West. Carl had long been fascinated with horses and wide open spaces—and in his mind, the two went together.

As he leaned his bicycle up against the building, he remembered the time he'd been invited to the Uelands' family home a few miles out of the city. There he was allowed to ride the horse that belonged to the Ueland boys, Torvald and Rolf. Riding that horse through the pastures was like a dream come true. He'd never forgotten the sublime sensation of being in the saddle and the wonderful aromas of leather and horse mingled together.

Deep in thought, he failed to watch where he was going, and as he turned around, he ran smack into someone. A girl someone.

"Excuse me," he mumbled. "I wasn't watching. So sorry."

"Oh, that's all right. I'm not hurt," said the dark-haired girl. "Well, Carlton," she added. "Hello."

Carl, knowing his ears were red as beets, tipped his cap. The girl, Jillian Oliver, was from his class at school. "Hello, Jillian," he said, his voice cracking.

"How nice to see you." Jillian always spoke kindly to people. Her dark hair lay about her shoulders in soft ringlets, looking glossy against her lavender dress. Her large brown eyes were wide, and across her nose lay a smattering of freckles from the summer sun. "I haven't seen you since graduation night," she said. "Are you having a good summer?"

"Good enough, I suppose."

"Jillian!" came a sharp voice from behind them. "Watch who you're talking to." There stood Jillian's stocky older brother, Sidney. Beside him stood his pal, a hawk-faced boy named Weldon Pritchard.

"You don't wanna be keeping company with those dumb kraut-eaters," Weldon put in. "Come on," Sidney ordered. "The moving picture is about to start."

Jillian turned to go, but over her shoulder she said, "Nice to see you again, Carl."

Taking Jillian's arm, Sidney moved her to the other side of him as though Carl had a contagious disease. "If I catch you talking to my sister again, I'll rearrange your face."

"And I'll help him," Weldon snarled.

CHAPTER 3

General Pershing in France

Carl waited near his bicycle for the trio to go inside—and for his heart to stop banging against his chest—before purchasing his ticket. No sense in taking any chances.

The two boys were a grade ahead of Carl, and he could remember them as bullies on the playground at Washington Elementary picking on the younger kids. Next fall, when Carl was a freshman at Central, he'd be with them once again. Not a cheerful thought.

The theater was already darkened when he entered. Slipping into a seat near the back, he watched as the newsreels began to roll. The pianist in the front played rousing patriotic music as scenes of army training camps splashed on the white screen, showing row upon row of marching doughboys in their broad-brimmed peaked campaign hats, high collared blouses, and trousers with leggings that wrapped from ankle to shin. How smart they looked marching in perfect formation.

Another reel showed young men all across the country peacefully registering for the draft at their local polling places. These scenes proved the critics were wrong. Signing up for the draft had gone off without a hitch.

The next scene was of General John J. "Black Jack" Pershing, who was in command of the American Expeditionary Force. The ruggedly handsome man with a smart-looking gray mustache stood tall and proud in his uniform and military hat as he walked off the British liner *Baltic* and stepped onto French soil. General Pershing had gone over with a few staff officers and enlisted men to set up the command centers. Carl just knew Truman would have given anything to have been on that ship.

From there, the scene switched to wild jubilant crowds in Boulogne, where the French greeted the general. Crowds overflowed the sidewalks and leaned from the balconies overlooking the route. Women and children tossed flowers and bits of cloth to show their appreciation for the arrival of the Yanks, as the Americans were called.

Surely, Carl thought, it would be worth it all to help those people who had suffered so much at the hands of the enemy.

Enemy. The word wrenched inside him. How was one to figure out just who the enemy was? The Central Powers were made up of Austria-Hungary, Bulgaria, and the Ottoman Empire, which included the Turks. In spite of the fact that all those countries were fighting the Allies, Americans talked and acted as though Germans were the only ones being fought against.

Papa had said that during wartime all reason ceases. "But we continue to forgive and love," he said. Forgiving was so difficult when anger fumed inside Carl against people, like Sidney and Weldon, who thought they were so high and mighty.

Carl was thankful when the newsreels were over and the main attraction began. He could almost hear the pounding hoofbeats and taste the dust as the cowboys in their ten-gallon hats and shiny spurs rode gallantly across the screen. The cowboys courted danger, but the hero always thwarted the bad guys. By and by, he got the pretty girl as well.

Seeing the heroine batting her eyelashes at William S. Hart turned Carl's thoughts to Jillian Oliver. While she'd never been unfriendly to him at school, still she'd never really spoken to him much, either. He was surprised that she'd not spoken sharply to him when he nearly knocked her over. The starlet playing opposite Hart was pretty, but Carl, sitting in that dark theater all by himself, decided that Jillian Oliver was much prettier.

"I'll get a certificate for helping to gather scrap iron," Larry said. "And maybe even a badge." His voice vibrated as he bounced along, perched on the handlebars of Carl's bicycle. Larry's empty wagon rattled and clattered as it rolled along behind the bicycle. Larry had been quite impressed when Carl showed him how they could hook up the wagon to the bicycle.

"You're so smart," Larry told his older cousin.

Carl wasn't sure why he'd agreed to take Larry to the

dump to look for scrap iron. After all, Carl wasn't in the Boy Scouts. Larry probably could have gone with a bunch of boys from his own troop and done a fair job of scrounging. But Larry had asked Carl, and in a weak moment, Carl had agreed.

Mama had asked Carl one time if he wanted to join the Scouts. He knew that somehow she would have come up with the money to purchase his uniform if that's what he'd wanted. The uniforms were definitely a draw, but thinking of the problems he'd face as a German American—it simply wasn't worth it. So he declined.

Larry's wagon was good-sized, with sides made of wooden slats. After spending several long hours at the smelly dump by the river, the boys finally had the wagon filled with pieces of scrap iron.

"I knew I'd get it filled with you helping me," Larry said proudly.

The return trip wasn't so easy. Carl's legs were about ready to give out when he finally suggested that they unhook the wagon. From there, they took turns riding the bike while the other boy pulled the heavy wagon. By the time they returned to Larry's house, they were sweaty, dirty, and thirsty.

Aunt Frances told them that Edie and her friend Nell Swearingen were out for the day collecting peach pits. Red Cross volunteers across the city went from door to door asking housewives for peach pits. The pits were burned, and the special charcoal was then used as filters for gas masks. And gas masks saved the lives of soldiers in France when they faced an attack of poison gas from the enemy. Carl had seen the signs the girls carried with them. They read: *You Save Peach Seeds—They Will Save Soldiers' Lives.*

As Carl and Larry sat on the Allertons' front porch drinking glasses of cold lemonade that Aunt Frances had prepared, Carl thought about what Papa had told them last April after war was declared. Papa said that because of the war, their lives would be totally changed. He'd certainly been right. The war was touching every facet of their lives from gardens, to scrap iron, to peach pits.

Larry pointed at a house across the street. "See that red and white bunting hanging in the window over there?" he asked.

Carl nodded. He'd seen the service flags, as they were called, draped in windows all over the city. But he let Larry tell him about it.

"That blue star on the bunting means Greg Hastings has gone off to war. He left on the train just a few days ago." His young voice grew tight, almost choked. "I miss him a lot. He was a real good friend of mine. I sure hope he doesn't get hurt over there."

"Truman Vaught was a friend of mine," Carl told Larry, sensing what his younger cousin was feeling. "And I miss him, too."

"Truly?"

"Truly. And we pray for him every night."

That was all that was said. But Carl knew it probably helped Larry to know that someone else knew how he felt.

That evening, the families gathered together at the Allertons', as they did most every Saturday night. While they sat in the parlor, Uncle Richard—who was Dr. Richard Allerton to most of the neighbors—played his Victrola. A new song blared out: *Over there, over there. Oh, the Yanks are coming, the Yanks are coming, The Yanks are coming over there.*

Next came "Good-bye Broadway; Hello France." After it was finished playing, Uncle Richard said, "War is so terrible, the best thing we can do is sing about it to soften the blows."

Aunt Esther and Uncle Erik, who'd recently moved back to the city from a farm in Missouri, were talking intently with Aunt Frances about women's right to vote. Carl and Larry sat at the game table engrossed in a game of checkers. Larry was being soundly trounced.

"They've said for years that a woman's place was in the home," Aunt Frances was saying. "But look what's happening in England this very minute. All women—young and old, rich and poor, trained and untrained—are working in industry, in government departments, and as nurses. Hundreds more have volunteered for the Women's Army Auxiliary Corps. I'll not be surprised if it's the same way here in America very shortly."

"They can't use that tired old argument about keeping us at home after this," Aunt Esther agreed.

"If we help to win the war," Lydia put in, "then the vote should definitely be ours." Lydia was much like her two aunts in her outspoken opinions about women deserving the right to vote.

Carl noticed that Edie wasn't joining the discussion. She was sitting in the rocking chair with the youngest Allerton, four-year-old Harry, nearly asleep in her lap. Since she stayed with Harry so much, he was partial to her. Gloria, the middle child, was playing dolls on the floor with Aunt Esther's daughter, Adeline.

"Many of those women in the munitions factories risk their lives daily," Uncle Erik put in. As a newspaperman, Erik Moe knew a great deal about such things. "We've received reports of explosions where women workers have been blinded, maimed, or even killed. They're making as genuine a sacrifice as the men on the battlefield."

Carl glanced over at Edie and smiled. They were thinking the same thing. Everyone agreed about the issue, so why were they arguing so strongly?

"Well, I've decided to quit my job clerking in Woolworth's basement," Lydia blurted out boldly.

Mama, who was working on a piece of embroidery, stopped her needle in midair and looked up. Mama was seldom drawn into these conversations.

Lydia no doubt chose that moment to make her announcement so she'd have support from her aunts in case Mama disagreed. "And just what do you plan to do?" Mama asked quietly.

"I'm going to get a job sewing military uniforms in the garment factory. Then I'll be helping the war effort just like Aunt Frances said the women in Britain are doing."

Papa spoke up. "Lydia, in the fall if you are at Woolworth's, you can return to a part-time position. Not so at the garment factory."

"Then I'll just quit school," Lydia said.

Suddenly all the aunts and uncles as well as Mama and Papa were disagreeing with her.

"Some girls may have to quit school to go to work," Aunt Esther said, putting her hand on Lydia's shoulder. "But you will not be one of them as long as you have such hardworking parents."

"Ja," Papa said in agreement. "No more talk of not finishing school. We will not hear of it."

"King me," Carl said to Larry. Larry groaned as he placed one wooden checker on top of another. As their game continued, Carl thought about what Lydia had said. In the past few months, he, too, had considered quitting school. He wasn't the strong student that Tim was. Although he loved to read, he didn't much care about reading the books the teachers wanted him to read. He preferred reading what *he* wanted to read.

Truman Vaught had quit school when he was in the eighth grade, and he had had a good job at the Minneapolis *Tribune* and did well for himself. Carl was sure he could do the same thing. There would be plenty of jobs available now that the war had increased factory production. And if he left school, he'd no longer have to listen to all those jibes about being German.

But then, if he quit school, he'd not have many chances to see the brown-eyed Jillian again. Perhaps no chance at all. That wasn't too pleasing a thought.

"King me," Larry said, grinning broadly. "I don't know where your mind was, but you missed that move when it was plain as the nose on your face."

CHAPTER 4

Thrift Stamps

The early morning air was cool on Carl's face as he rode his bicycle downtown to the *Tribune* office building. Workers were cleaning the downtown streets of the trash left from the recent Fourth of July parade. Carl could hardly remember such a patriotic Fourth. More bands, more speeches, more flag-waving than ever before.

In the alley behind the *Tribune* office, crowds of newsboys were milling about waiting for their rope-bound bundles of papers. Several of the boys greeted Carl as he propped his bicycle against the fence that bordered the alley.

"What's the news?" Carl asked.

"Take a look," said Virgil Winkleman. Still a shorty at age nine, his name was almost as big as he was. All the other boys called him Winkie. Most of the youngsters who hawked papers on the street corners of downtown Minneapolis were orphans—street children with no real homes. And that included Winkie.

Carl took a copy of the *Tribune* from Winkie and saw the photographs of the doughboys in a triumphal parade down the streets of Paris. The 1st Division led by Pershing was marching down the Champs-Elysées in a grand and glorious Fourth of July celebration. Thousands lined the streets, the caption said, and were weeping, cheering, and applauding.

Many people threw flowers at the soldiers, and some broke into the lines and gave the doughboys gifts. Although the newspaper photographs were not as dramatic as a newsreel, Carl couldn't mistake the overwhelming joy displayed by the French people. Hope had been restored to them when American troops marched down their streets.

"My friend Truman Vaught may be in that parade," Carl said pointing at the photo.

"Honest?" Winkie said. "You know a real soldier?"

"Before this war's over," said a skinny boy known as Stilt, "everyone in the nation will know a soldier."

Carl was impressed by Stilt's wisdom. Papa had said nearly the same thing. "It won't be long," Papa had said, "before they'll be calling for boys who are younger than twenty-one. All our finest young men will march off to war." Carl preferred to believe the war would be over long before that happened.

"How are you gonna word your call?" Winkie asked Stilt, looking up at his taller friend.

"I dunno. Some of them French names are hard to pronounce."

"Don't use the street name," Carl suggested. "Just say Paris. Everyone knows about Paris."

"Extra! Extra! Read all about it!" Stilt chanted. "Doughboys greeted by cheering French on Paris streets!"

"That'll sell," Carl told him.

The boys loaded up their papers in their canvas bags and went off to their corners. Since Carl threw his papers onto the front porches of his customers, all his papers had to be folded before he left to cover his route. It took two canvas bags to hold them all.

Carl first started carrying a route when he was only ten, following along behind Timothy. Even Lydia had helped the boys for a time. Now it was all his. Carl had enlarged his route nearly every year with good customers who seemed to trust and appreciate him. At least they paid their bills on time—that's what mattered most.

By the time his bags were empty, the sun was breaking through the treetops and the early morning coolness was quickly making way for another very hot July day. The summer heat made Carl's victory garden more and more demanding. It seemed he did nothing but weed, till, and water day after day.

Instead of riding home, Carl turned his bicycle back toward downtown. He'd seen a garden sprinkler in the window of Marienhof's Hardware Store. The gadget had four little prongs that stuck up and whirled around, slinging water every which way. He planned to hook that sprinkler onto the end of the black rubber hose that he and Papa had purchased last spring. The sprinkler could be just the thing to keep his garden flourishing.

It took only a minute to go inside and make his purchase. He was in a hurry to get home to the breakfast Edie was cooking. His stomach was growling something fierce. Carl knew she was fixing dried apples and sausage buttons, one of his favorites. When he was very small he remembered Papa calling it *Schnitz und Knopfen*, but of course no one dared speak German words these days. Not even at home.

After leaving the store with his purchase, Carl had barely ridden a block when he saw Sidney Oliver and Weldon Pritchard swaggering toward him, all decked out in their starched and creased khaki-colored Boy Scout uniforms. They were in fine form from their peaked hats to their spit-shined oxfords. Had he seen them a minute sooner, Carl could have easily turned and gone down another street. But it was too late.

Both boys hurried toward him and grabbed at the handlebars of his bicycle. "Hey there, Schmidt," Sidney said. "You're just the fellow we're looking for."

"That's right," Weldon echoed, his mouth curved into a smirk. "We're out selling Thrift Stamps this morning, and every good little patriotic boy should buy several cards of them."

Carl landed his feet on the ground and attempted to wrench the handlebars from Sidney's grasp, but the boy was too strong for him. "I bought stamps just a couple weeks ago," he said, "from my cousin, Larry Allerton."

"Do you think we're going to take the word of a Hun on that?" Sidney laughed. "What do you take us for? No one believes a man-eating Hun."

"Not even another Hun," Weldon wisecracked.

Carl dug into the pocket of his trousers. "I have my liberty button right here." He'd also received a receipt from Larry, but he didn't bother to carry *that* around. Both the receipt and the card full of stamps were lying on top of the bureau in his bedroom. Who'd have thought he needed to carry them around? The thought of kowtowing to these two mindless fellows filled Carl with disgust.

"Buttons don't prove anything," Sidney said, scorning the object lying in Carl's palm. "You mighta picked that up on the ground where someone dropped it."

Weldon snatched the button from his hand.

"Hey," Carl said, "give that back."

"Twenty-five cents for the Thrift Stamps, and I'll let you have the button back to boot."

There was nothing Carl could do but pull out the quarter from his pocket and pay them. The money was the change from his purchase at the hardware store. He'd have to skip a movie this week.

"Now see, Sidney," Weldon said. "See how cooperative a Hun can be when you know how to handle him?"

When he took the quarter, Weldon let go of the bicycle. Carl stuffed the stamps and button into his pocket, pushed off, and rode away as fast as he could, the sound of their laughter taunting him for blocks.

By the time he arrived home, all the family members had left for work. Edie was in the kitchen looking terribly upset. Carl said nothing about what had just happened to him. His sister took his plate of sausage and apples from the warming oven as Frosty circled in figure eights around her legs.

"What took you so long?" she asked absently.

He held up the sprinkler. "I stopped at the hardware store."

Nodding, she turned back to the sink where she was

scrubbing the breakfast dishes. Frosty followed and continued rubbing against her legs.

"Is everything all right?" Carl asked.

She pointed to the cabinet where loaves of bread were covered with a tea towel. "Just look at that."

He lifted the towel, expecting to see the high light golden loaves that Edie usually pulled from the oven when she baked bread. Instead they were small and hard. "What is it?"

"Liberty bread."

"Liberty bread?"

Edie nodded. "My small contribution to the war effort."

Carl wasn't sure what to say. Edie was always so proud of her culinary creations. "What made it like that?"

"I followed the recipe. The recipe given out by the Food Production and Conservation Committee." She lifted the towel and looked forlornly at the loaves. "The amount of flour is cut back and substituted with rolled oats. But the rolled oats soak up more of the liquid, so the liquid must be increased. Something tells me they didn't take much care to try this recipe out before they decided to tell us to use it." She tapped the top of a loaf and it sounded hard as a rock.

Carl sat down at the table to eat. "If I'd known, I could have purchased a saw at the hardware store for you."

She smiled ruefully and turned back to her dishes. "What was in the news?"

Carl always brought a copy of the newspaper home. He pulled it from his back pocket and spread it out on the table. "Our troops were parading in Paris."

Edie wiped her dripping soapy hands and came to look. "Paris. Imagine that. All our boys over there so far away."

"And so much closer to all the fighting," Carl said.

Edie paused. "Nell's brother, Devlin, could be right there

in that picture somewhere." She touched the photo of the marching troops being cheered by the thousands of Parisians.

"And Truman as well."

She nodded. "I guess hard loaves of bread are a small thing compared to being shot at."

So, Carl thought, *is being harassed by two rowdies like Sidney and Weldon.* But the anger continued to seethe inside him. Mostly it was anger at himself for not standing up to them.

CHAPTER 5

The Root Cellar

The family's next letter from Truman told them about training in France and included high praise for Black Jack Pershing.

> *It seems the French and British assumed they'd just suck us right into their existing troop formations, but good old Black Jack wouldn't hear of it. Know what he told them? The general said, "We came American. We shall remain American and go into battle with Old Glory over our heads. I will not parcel out American boys!"*

*Were we ever proud of him. We didn't come
over here to simply be replacements for the dying
Allies. We came to fight as one force, and thanks to
Black Jack's stand, that's what will happen.*

*I may not be able to write as many letters now.
We're in the most grueling training you can imagine. Camp Sheridan was a Sunday school picnic in
comparison.*

*All of us are aware that some may not come
home. But better that we die over here than for war
to come to your doorstep.*

"They're dying to protect us," Edie whispered when
Tim finished reading the letter. "It's almost like Jesus sacri-
ficing Himself on the cross for us. It may not purchase sal-
vation, but it might purchase our safety and freedom."

Lydia sat with her handkerchief pressed hard against her
mouth. She could hardly bear it when Truman's letters
spoke of dying. Often after a letter was read, she would go
outside and take a long walk. Mama and Papa advised the
rest of them not to bother her, but to cheer her up as much
as possible.

Carl wondered what it might be like if Tim were called
to serve. He wasn't quite old enough yet, but if the draft age
were lowered, it could happen. None of them ever talked
about it openly, but Carl knew it was on everyone's mind.

While the Minneapolis Women's Suffrage Association eased
off their work that summer in order to tend to war efforts, suf-
fragettes in Washington, D.C., threw their actions into high
gear. Groups of women picketed right outside the gates of the
White House. Many were arrested and thrown into jail.

While Papa was all for women voting, Carl could tell he wasn't too sure about these actions. They followed the newspaper coverage closely. As the summer progressed, the imprisoned women staged a hunger strike. Carl was amazed. How could anyone go without eating? On purpose?

When the Schmidts, the Moes, and the Allertons got together, this turn of events provided a new topic of conversation. Whereas previously they had all agreed, now there were differing points of view.

"Clara feels it's too extreme," Aunt Frances said. She was talking about Clara Ueland, who headed up the suffrage groups in the state of Minnesota. Aunt Frances had worked closely with Mrs. Ueland, and the two were dear friends. "If Clara says it's too extreme, then I agree with her."

"Well I don't." This from Lydia.

They were sitting out on the Allertons' front porch, enjoying the evening breeze as it swept away the heat of the day. The younger cousins were out playing in the yard. Their carefree squeals and laughter floated out across the night air.

Carl couldn't believe Lydia would disagree with Mrs. Ueland. All of them knew how much Lydia respected the entire Ueland family.

"Tell us, Lydia," Uncle Erik said. "What's your opinion about all this?" Uncle Erik's eyes twinkled as he toyed with his handlebar mustache. He always seemed a bit amused by Lydia's outspokenness, and he enjoyed egging her on.

"I believe the picketing and the hunger strikes are exactly what's needed to finally sway the public to our side. Nothing else has worked. So why oppose these drastic measures when they just might be the answer?"

"She may be right," Uncle Erik said. "I read that even Minnesota's senator Charles Lindbergh wrote a letter to

President Wilson, protesting the horrid treatment of the women in the prisons."

"Just because he protested their treatment," Aunt Esther put in, "doesn't mean he agrees with what they did to be placed in jail in the first place."

The conversation swirled around endlessly as Carl sat listening. Everyone seemed to have an opinion but him. How he wished he could go off by himself and spend hours with his camera and developing trays like he'd done before Truman went away.

When the snap beans came on, Mama and the girls stayed up canning late into the night. Mama said Edie shouldn't have to do that big job all by herself. The whole house smelled like beans, but no one complained. After the beans, they put up jars of tomatoes and pickled beets. Carl kept having to go to the store and buy more canning jars. Then in late August, Papa decided they should dig a root cellar.

"Bruno next door has one," he said, smoothing his mustache, which recently had become flecked with gray. "I've been thinking that might be the best way to preserve the potatoes, onions, and turnips. No sense in Carl working hard to grow all these vegetables if we just let them spoil."

Carl almost groaned out loud. Dig a root cellar? That sounded way beyond what they were supposed to be doing for the war. But once Papa made up his mind, there was no talking him out of it.

When Papa discussed the matter with Bruno, their neighbor not only volunteered to help, but brought along two of his husky sons as well. The two sons were men with families of their own. Tim told Carl privately that he thought Papa would never have mentioned the idea to

Bruno if he'd known all these Germans would be converging on their backyard.

When the war first began three years ago, Bruno Bierschwale had been one of the vocal German Americans, speaking out in behalf of Germany and differing with the American government on selling munitions to the Allies. Carl could remember back then when Bruno was a big strong man with a powerfully gruff voice. Now he looked old and stoop-shouldered. He'd suffered much at the hands of persecutors. His leather goods shop had twice been splashed with yellow paint and ransacked once. It never caused him to close the doors of the shop, but the incidents had taken a terrible toll on his health.

Every night when Bruno and his sons got off work, they manned shovels and worked on the Schmidts' root cellar until it was too dark to see. Bruno taught Papa how to reinforce the sides with timbers to hold it firm and how to line the floor with stones to make a suitable flooring. The room wouldn't be very large—just big enough to store the larder from the family's garden harvest.

"Shelves we build for to hold Frau Schmidt's jars of canning," Bruno told them. Shaking his head he said, "Good Germans should always haff gardens. Vas always the vay in the old country."

Carl glanced at Tim, and they both rolled their eyes. What Mr. Bierschwale remembered as the old country was virtually nonexistent now. Carl and Tim both knew that civilians in Germany were going without food as the war dragged on and on.

"*Schrecklich! Schrecklich*! How the Americans waste," Mr. Bierschwale continued, shaking his head. "At the stores paying money for what grows free from soil."

Carl knew enough German to know he was saying it was *dreadful, dreadful.* It made Carl more than a little nervous to hear Mr. Bierschwale's German words booming out as they worked in the yard. But what was worse, his two burly sons joined right in.

One evening Carl had gone inside the house to tell Mama the men were ready for a water break. Mama and the girls were making jars of tomato sauce, and a big kettle was boiling on the stove, giving off a delicious tangy aroma.

"I'll fetch it," Lydia offered, taking down mugs from the cabinet.

Just then a knock sounded at the front door. Mama went to answer it. Carl could plainly hear the man's voice saying, "My name is Maurice Perkins. I'm from the Liberty Bonds Town Committee. I'd like to talk to the man of the house about your commitment to purchase liberty bonds for the war effort."

Carl heard Mama pause a moment. "He's in the back-yard," she said. "I'll go get him."

"No need, ma'am," the man answered. "I'll just go back myself."

Carl slipped out to the porch stoop to listen. Mama pushed past him to call softly to Papa, warning him of the official's approach. Carl saw Papa nod.

Maurice Perkins stopped a moment and assessed the work in progress. He was a small man dressed in a natty suit with a starched collar and necktie. "What's going on here? An excavation?" His attempt at humor was lost on Bruno Bierschwale.

"Any dumb ox sees it is root cellar," he said. "We grow government victory garden vegetables. We store dem in der cellar."

The man eyed Mr. Bierschwale suspiciously. "Are you Mr. Schmidt?" he asked.

"I'm Hans Schmidt," Papa said, stepping forward.

Mama appeared then, carrying a tray of her nicest glasses full of water—with ice—serving the official first.

Carl kept back and watched as Mr. Perkins looked around at the younger Bierschwale men. To Papa he said, "You're president of the local mill workers union. Is that correct?"

"That is correct," Papa said.

"I'm here to talk to you about your commitment to the liberty bond fund. I'm sure you've been considering what your purchase will be."

Papa nodded. "I have."

"Iss un-American to require such money," Mr. Bierschwale spoke up, "without they make a vote to it first."

Maurice Perkins studied the big German through narrowed eyes.

The two younger Bierschwales stood leaning on their shovels and drinking their cold water. "Ja," said one in agreement with his father. "Ja, iss true," chorused the second.

Carl couldn't believe his ears. Didn't they know when to keep quiet? These officials were able to report back to the Commission of Public Safety, whose job it was to uncover traitors and locate those who in any way opposed the cause of the war.

"If you come back tomorrow evening, I will set aside time to speak with you," Papa offered in his gentle way.

"Over there, I live," Bruno said, pointing to his bungalow next door, which was almost identical in size and shape to the Schmidts'. "No good for you to come. Whether I buy bonds yet, I do not know."

Mr. Perkins turned his back on Mr. Bierschwale. To Papa, he said, "This looks like a neighborhood that will bear close surveillance." He tipped his hat. "I'll be here tomorrow evening at the same time. I expect you to be ready."

"I'll be ready," Papa said.

"I'll swear," Carl said, stepping back into the kitchen, "old Bruno's gonna cause trouble for the whole lot of us."

"Please don't swear," Mama said quietly. "We cannot control Bruno Bierschwale, and we must let him think for himself, such as we'd expect others to do for us."

"In this day and time," Lydia said as she lifted a scalding canning jar from a kettle of boiling water, "we seem to have very little right to think for ourselves, either."

Carl agreed with Lydia. And even though he didn't feel that Mr. Bierschwale needed to be quite so vocal, something deep inside him admired the old man for his courage.

One of the first things that caught Carl's attention when he stepped into the halls of Central High School as a freshman in September was a big sign on the wall:

Don't Be SUSPECTED!
Use American Language
America Is Our Home

All immigrants were being trained to become full-fledged Americans as quickly as possible, as though it were possible to remove in a matter of days all that they'd learned in a lifetime in some other country. Carl felt particularly sorry for the newly arrived German children whose accents were still very strong.

Just as Mama and Papa had declared, Lydia had not been

allowed to quit school, and she was still employed at Woolworth's. The fact that his bold, daring sister was attending his school gave Carl a sense of feeling protected, although he wouldn't have admitted it to anyone. He certainly didn't want to be accused of hiding behind her skirts.

The first month of school was a blur. What with finishing the root cellar, helping Papa build the big double doors for the cellar and the frame that held them, harvesting the garden, and continuing his large paper route, there were times Carl could barely hold his eyes open in class.

There'd been little in elementary school to prepare him for the rigors of high school. Only because of his older siblings had he become familiar with the need to hurry from class to class with only a few minutes to grab his book at the metal lockers that lined the hallways.

Jillian Oliver's locker was only a short way down the hall from Carl's. Each morning she would say good morning to him. He'd mumble a reply and hurry on his way. His response bordered on rudeness, but he certainly didn't want to have another run-in with her older brother and his mouthy sidekick. Perhaps the leathery old Bruno Bierschwale could act like a bold hero, but Carl wasn't made of that kind of stuff.

CHAPTER 6

Papa's Arrest

The leaves on the trees were growing crimson and gold and drifting lazily to the ground when news came of the first American deaths in the war. Suddenly all the rousing march songs and all the fine parades faded into vague memory. The reality of war slammed home.

Carl hurried home from his route to show Papa and the rest of the family the headlines. On November 2, Company F, 2nd Battalion, 16th U.S. Infantry were in the trenches near Bathelémont when shells from eight-inch mortars blasted their position. As the Schmidt family crowded around the breakfast table, Carl read the details:

> *Under cover of the bombardment, a 100-man German assault troop, the dread* Stosstruppen, *launched a vicious hit-and-run raid. It lasted only three minutes. When it was over, three Americans lay dead in the muddy trench; eleven missing, a sergeant and ten men taken prisoner.*

Carl went on to read the names and hometowns of the three slain Americans. One was from Indiana, one from Pennsylvania, and the third from Iowa.

"Now the grieving begins," Papa said solemnly as he stood and pulled on his coat. "This is what war is truly all about."

Also in November came news of a frightening revolution in Russia. Demonstrations and strikes in Petrograd had exploded into open revolution. Czar Nicholas II abdicated the throne, and now the Bolsheviks were in power. Carl wondered how the Russians could continue to help fight the Germans when they were fighting one another. It was as though the whole world had gone crazy.

It was Thanksgiving before they heard from Truman again. Now he was in the trenches. After all his trips by ambulance when serving in the American Field Ambulance, he was finally where he'd longed to be—in the midst of the fighting. They could tell by his letter that it was far more gruesome than he'd ever imagined:

> *I've heard a million stories about the trenches but never dreamed it could be this horrible. We*

live in the dark with the snails. Sometimes we have flickering candlelight, but often the air is so foul not even a candle will remain burning.

When it rains—which it seems to do constantly— the sides of the trenches sometimes cave in. The snails are the least of our worries. It's the trench rats that are a constant concern. They can shred shoe leather like tender lettuce. And then there're the cooties. No soldier is immune from being a warm home to a vast host of these horrid lice!

A few days of this sitting and sitting and sitting, and one almost prays for zero hour and an attack against the Hun!

When Carl went to sleep in his warm, dry, safe bed that night, he couldn't stop thinking about his friend Truman sitting wet and cold in a lonely trench in France with rats chewing his boots and lice biting his body. It kept sleep away for hours.

Papa liked to joke about their root cellar. "Every time we fetch a potato, a carrot, or a turnip from the cellar, I feel almost like a rugged homesteader out there on the Minnesota prairies," he told them. "It makes me very proud of my family to think of all we've done with the garden and the food preservation."

And not one of them complained when a jar of spicy pickled beets was opened or a mess of snap beans cooked up with bits of ham stirred in.

When Edie served the snap beans, she asked the family if they felt she'd disobeyed the porkless or meatless day. Her question became a joke with the family because there were so few little pieces of meat in the beans. The Food Administration, headed up in Washington, D.C., by a man named Herbert Hoover, had declared a voluntary food rationing plan. Mondays and Wednesdays were wheatless, Tuesdays were meatless, and Thursdays and Saturdays were porkless. Papa said the plan made Americans everywhere thankful to see Friday come.

Then came the gasless Sundays, when the nation of automobile drivers were asked to leave their Tin Lizzies at home and take the trolleys or walk. All in the name of the war!

Some, like Uncle Richard, called Mr. Hoover a food dictator because he controlled what farmers produced, how much food stayed in the U.S., and how much went to the Allies. He also decided how much the grocery stores could charge their customers.

Uncle Erik, however, supported the job Herbert Hoover was doing. "If Hoover could handle the feeding of the entire nation of Belgium by way of the Commission for Relief in Belgium, then he can do this job just as well."

No matter where a person went in the fall of 1917, there were posters, signs, and banners telling of Hoover's national program. *Feed a Fighter! Eat only what you need—waste nothing*! declared one sign posted at the grocery store. The illustration was of a doughboy sitting in a trench.

Another sign was tacked to the side of a delivery dray. It showed three women pulling a plow in a field. The caption asked, *Will you help the women of France? SAVE WHEAT!*

As the war efforts at home increased, so did the feelings against Germans and anything that had to do with Germans. Lydia's favorite German language teacher at the high school was fired with no explanation. Several towns and cities across the nation with German-sounding names were changing them. Germantown, Nebraska, became Garland; Berlin, Iowa, became Lincoln; East Germantown, Indiana, became Pershing.

Citizens were instructed to call sauerkraut "liberty cabbage." Because Hamburg was the name of a German city, ground beef patties were to be called "liberty steaks" instead of hamburgers.

One day in history class, Carl opened his book to see that part of a page had been clipped out. Later he learned it was a short section that spoke of Kaiser Wilhelm as an honest schoolboy.

Edie came home from school to say that all the German folk songs had been clipped from her music book. The Schmidts wondered how much more prejudice there could be, and where—or when—it would all end.

On a cold, gray December afternoon, Carl had ridden his bicycle to the Allertons' to help Larry fetch another load of scrap iron. Since everyone was gathering scrap iron, it wasn't as easy to find as it had once been. But regardless, Carl had agreed to go with Larry to the dump.

When they returned home, Larry showed Carl the packets of pamphlets he'd received from his Scout leader. The first was entitled, "How the War Came to America." It explained how to be constantly on the watch for German spies. A second pamphlet contained the shocking title, "Why We Hate Germany."

"Of course that doesn't mean *you*," Larry said, acting as though the words meant nothing. "But," he continued, "I have to persuade fifteen influential adults in my neighborhood to distribute these pamphlets. When I do, I'll get yet another badge."

As Carl rode his bicycle homeward from the Allertons', he thought about the pamphlets. Larry wanted to earn his badges and be a good and loyal Boy Scout, and Carl couldn't blame him for that. But it was amazing how totally different circumstances were for him and his cousin. Larry would never know the sickening feeling of being taunted and tormented and discriminated against just because of his name.

The next morning, Carl woke up before dawn. He could tell there'd been a big snow before he looked out the window. The wind ripped at the eaves of the house, making the boards creak and groan. He'd need to pull on an extra pair of woolen long-johns to endure the cold.

As Carl rummaged through the drawer in the darkness, Tim turned on the bedside lamp. "Want some help this morning?"

Carl grinned. "I won't refuse an offer."

In spite of the fact that Tim worked all day at an engineering office and attended classes at night, he was still willing to pitch in and help Carl with the route when the weather turned nasty.

Later, as the two of them tromped through the blowing snow, slapping themselves to keep warm, Carl knew that in spite of all the bad things that were happening, he was very blessed to have such a kind and caring older brother.

Mama always said she could set the cuckoo clock in the parlor by Papa's arrival home from work. So that evening when he was late, they were all concerned.

Earlier Tim and Carl had gone out to shovel snow off the doors of the root cellar and brought in enough vegetables for Edie to use for the next several days. It was cozy and dry in the cellar.

"If you'd been thinking correctly," Tim had teased Carl, "you and Papa could have made this cellar large enough for you to put your darkroom down here. No light would get in this place."

They waited supper until the cuckoo sounded seven-thirty, then Mama said, "We'll eat now. Papa will be along soon. It's probably just the snow. Perhaps he's found some-one who needed a helping hand."

Her voice was steady, but Carl could read the concern in her eyes. Across the nation, pressure was mounting for unions to disband. Some people charged that union leaders were being paid by the Kaiser to slow down production in the factories. That would hurt the Allies in the war. And Papa was a union officer with a German name.

Conversation during supper was stilted. The minutes dragged slowly by, and no one really wanted to eat. When the telephone abruptly rang, everyone jumped.

Mama slowly rose to answer it. They watched her face grow pale. "Yes, this is Mrs. Hans Schmidt," she said. Then, "Why?" and "Where is he?" A few more comments were exchanged, and she hung up.

Turning to the family, she said, "Get your coats and boots. We're going downtown. Your papa's been arrested."

CHAPTER 7

Jail Visit

"Why's Papa in jail?" Edie asked, her eyes wide. Frosty had crawled up into her arms, and she was clutching the cat tightly.

"He's been accused of sabotage at the mill."

"Sabotage?" Tim was on his feet, helping Mama into her coat. "What kind of sabotage?"

"They claim someone has put ground glass into the flour. They say it was your papa."

"I knew that solicitor, Mr. Perkins, who came in August would make trouble," Lydia said, grabbing for her own coat and knitted wool hat. "I could tell by the look in his eye."

"We know nothing of the sort, Lydia," Mama said firmly. "That's not how Papa would have us talk at this moment."

Carl's feet felt like lead as he moved in a daze to the hooks by the door where the coats hung. "Papa in jail? He'd never hurt even a little flea."

"We know that," Mama said. "But they don't know that."

"What're we going to do?" Edie asked.

"We'll know when we get there," Mama answered as she led them out the door into the fierce blowing snow.

The snow was deep on the ground and thick in the air. Carl grabbed hold of Edie's hand and steadied her as they pushed forward to get to the trolley stop. They could barely see the soft glow of the street lamps through the swirling snow. No one said a word as they moved in a straight line to the trolley stop. Carl wondered if the trolleys were even running. When the snow became too deep, the trolleys simply shut down.

By the time they reached the trolley stop, there was no feeling in Carl's toes. He was worried about Mama and the girls. The five of them stood in a tight cluster, hardly moving.

"How long should we wait?" Tim asked Mama, raising his voice to be heard over the harsh wind.

"We'll know," Mama answered.

"Maybe we should have called Uncle Richard," Lydia said.

Mama shook her head. "Not unless we have to."

After what seemed like an eternity, but was really only a few moments, they heard the welcome sound of the trolley's clanging bell. Then they could make out the golden lights of the car as it moved slowly, cautiously down the tracks.

Surprise registered on the conductor's face when the trolley came to a stop and the door opened. They were met with a welcome rush of warm air as they boarded.

"Nasty night for you folks to be out and about."

Mama nodded and was fishing about in her bag for the money, when Tim pulled it out of his pocket and paid all the fares. Carl knew how important every penny was to Tim now that he was paying for his college classes.

The trolley barely inched along the route. "The plows will be out directly," the conductor told them. "This will be our last run until the tracks can be cleared."

The Schmidts remained silent as they rode toward the courthouse downtown. Carl had never known such fear as was pounding in his head and chest at that moment. They'd all heard stories of beatings and even lynchings of union men. Could that happen to Papa? Right here in this city?

Two blocks from the courthouse, the trolley ground to a slow stop. "She's stuck," called out the conductor. "They'll be here in a few minutes to shovel us out. Want to wait? It'll be warmer in here."

Mama shook her head. "We'll walk." She stood and led them out like a row of ducklings—back out into the blowing storm.

Carl grabbed Edie's hand. Tim took the lead, breaking a path through the snow for Mama and Lydia. By the time they reached the courthouse, they were breathless and chilled to the bone.

Inside the marble-and-brass lobby, the sounds of their footsteps echoed back at them. Tim glanced over at the information desk. A man watched them warily.

"Let me talk to him, Mama," Tim whispered.

That whisper seemed to bounce and echo around the

room about fifty times. Carl watched as Tim boldly strode across the ornate lobby and stepped up to the desk as though he owned the place. How Carl wished he'd been given just a fraction of his brother's boldness.

Presently Tim returned and pointed to the elevator. "Come this way. The jail's on the eighth floor."

The difference between the first floor entrance and the eighth floor jail was like night and day. No spit-and-polish here. Only plain milky-colored walls with peeling paint, wooden floors, and bare lightbulbs hanging from the ceiling. This was not the place for a city to waste money on appearances. Again Tim stepped forward to speak to a sour-faced uniformed guard hunched over a cluttered desk.

"We've come to see Hans Schmidt," he said. There was not a bit of wavering in his voice.

The guard eyed them coolly. "All of you?"

"All of us," Tim answered without looking at Mama for an answer.

"Let me ask," the man said. Picking up the pedestal telephone on his desk, he whirled his chair around and talked to someone as though it were none of their business what he said. Yet they could hear every word. "Yeah," he was saying, "the whole blessed family's here. Came through the snowstorm, I guess."

He hooked the receiver into the holder and turned back around. "For a few minutes, Chief says."

Carl felt Edie move closer to him. He put his arm around her shoulder, but he was as frightened as she was.

Another guard was called in to unlock a metal door that opened on a hallway with a long row of cells on either side. Cramped little cages is all they were. Papa was at the end in the very last cell. As they moved past the men who were caged there, the prisoners called out hoots and taunts—especially at Lydia, who was a very pretty girl.

Tim put his arm about Lydia's waist and guided her quickly through the noise. The guard ahead of them called out, "Schmidt! Look lively there. Visitors."

He stopped in front of the cell. Papa looked calm, but sad. He was sitting on the cot. His face lit up at the sight of them. "Anna," he said almost in a whisper. "This awful storm."

"It's nothing," Mama said, reaching through the bar to take his hands.

"Children," Papa said, looking at each one of them, "thank you for coming together."

"What happened?" Tim asked.

Briefly Papa explained that he knew nothing until two policemen walked up to him at the gate as he left to go home after work. He wasn't told why he was being arrested. "After we arrived here, I was questioned about putting ground glass into the flour bins. It was not pleasant," he added.

Carl could only imagine the accusations that had been leveled at Papa, both for being German and for being union president.

"Have they set bail?" Tim asked.

Papa shook his head. "Not until tomorrow morning, they said. Because of the blizzard."

"I'll call Richard," Mama said. "About the bail money."

Carl could tell that bothered Papa deeply. Their papa never liked to look to anyone else for help. Even though the Allertons were a good deal wealthier than he, it never seemed to bother Papa a bit. He was proud of his job. But now. . .

"Whatever you feel is right, Anna," he said softly.

"We may have to call Uncle Richard anyway," Tim put in. "They're having trouble keeping the trolley tracks cleared in this storm. If he's not out on a call, we'll need him to drive us home."

Papa nodded.

Just then the guard yelled, "Time's up!" as though everyone in the cellblock were deaf.

Papa reached out to draw Mama's face nearer the bars and kissed her wet cheeks. Each of them reached through to touch him and hold him. How, Carl wondered, could they just walk out and leave Papa there alone with all those terrible men?

Suddenly the guard was ushering them out almost forcefully.

"Come back and see me again, sweetie," one of the inmates called to Lydia, as he reached out through the bars to try to touch her. Tim moved around to protect her and to hurry them out.

The metal door slammed behind them with frightening finality. Carl looked at it in disbelief. It was impossible that Papa could be on the other side of that heavy locked metal door.

"May we use your telephone?" Mama asked the guard at the desk.

"What do you think this is, a hotel?" he answered. "We can't have this line tied up. Important calls come through here. Go down and use the one in the lobby."

"Come on, Mama," Tim said, ushering them out of the office and down to the elevator.

Tim called Uncle Richard. Aunt Frances told him that their uncle was out on a call. Fortunately, he was near the downtown area, and fortunately she was able to call him and let him know their plight.

When Uncle Richard strode into that courthouse lobby, one would have thought lightning had just struck the building. He was fuming.

"Timothy, Carlton!" he said brusquely. "Come with me. Anna, you and the girls stay down here."

When they were upstairs again, Uncle Richard told the guard in no uncertain terms that he was there to post bail for Hans Schmidt and to get him out that very moment. "This man is not a threat to anyone's safety," Uncle Richard said, "and I want to talk to any person in this city who says he is."

It was obvious Dr. Richard Allerton's forthright manner had ruffled the feathers of the guard, but in spite of everything, the guard's hands were tied. No bail would be set until the next morning.

Almost nose-to-nose with the guard, Uncle Richard said, "I'm taking his family safely home. Then I'm coming back up here, and I'm not leaving until I walk out of here with Hans Schmidt by my side. Do you understand?"

"Yes, sir, Dr. Allerton," the man said softly.

While none of them ever wished to involve their relatives in such a terrible situation, Carl was glad to see Uncle Richard in action. It felt delicious.

"Terrific" is how Tim described Uncle Richard once they were home again safe and dry.

"Amazing and incredible," Carl added.

Both boys tried to convince Uncle Richard to allow them to stay at the courthouse with him. But he said they were needed at home to take care of Mama and their sisters.

None of them had spent even one night without Papa near them. It was an eerie feeling to be home without him.

After their prayer time and scripture reading, they all went to bed. But Carl was sure Mama was sitting up doing her embroidery.

"Tim," Carl said into the darkness of their bedroom.

"Yes?"

"You were as terrific tonight as Uncle Richard."

Carl heard Tim draw a deep breath. "Thank you, Carl. I didn't feel very terrific. I was pretty scared."

Carl thought about his brother's words for a long time as he listened to the wind beating against the house. At last he fell asleep.

CHAPTER 8

Banning Books

Even after Papa was released from jail, he was ordered to come to the courthouse time after time to answer ridiculous questions. Federal officials were called in on the case. Every hour that Papa spent away from his foreman's job was docked from his paycheck.

It made for a meager Christmas. But after what they'd experienced, no one cared about presents. What saddened Carl the most was to hear Papa promising Uncle Richard that he would pay back every penny of the bail money. Such a thing should never have happened!

During their prayer times, Papa kept bringing the family back to Matthew 5, where Jesus said, "Blessed are ye, when men shall revile you, and persecute you, and shall say all manner of evil against you falsely, for my sake. Rejoice and be exceeding glad: for great is your reward in heaven. . . ."

Then Papa would talk to them about making forgiveness a daily exercise.

"If you make a place in your heart for hate," he said, "what will you do with it when the war is over? Best not to let it in at all."

Sometimes Carl thought he had forgiven all the horrible things that had been done to him, but then something would happen that made him want to get even all over again. People were imagining all kinds of spy activity was going on. Some claimed that German submarines landed on U.S. shores at night and unloaded dozens of German spies who went about the country doing evil things.

Then Carl read a newspaper article where a government official suggested they put all German Americans into concentration camps in order to keep the country safe from spies. Surely such a thing could never happen in the United States of America!

But as the war got worse, the hatred increased. Songs by German composers were banned. People said, "German music is the most dangerous because it appeals to the emotions."

Then several famous German conductors were fired from their prestigious positions at major orchestras. One was even jailed.

Uncle Erik was one of the few who spoke out against the "Teutonic hysteria," as he called it. Several of his columns in the *Tribune* spoke clearly against such muddled thinking.

"We're losing sight of what our clear objectives are," he wrote.

But his was one tiny voice calling in the wilderness. Anyway, that's how Papa described it. "Most people find it easier to hate and suspect than to love and forgive," he told them.

A newsreel at the pictures gave Carl nightmares for days. It showed the city of Paris being shelled by some strange, monstrous German gun they called "Big Bertha." A letter from Truman told more details about the dreadful gun. As impossible as it seemed, this gun could shoot more than seventy-five miles with incredible accuracy, and it was shelling the innocent civilian population of Paris! Truman wrote:

> We're told that the citizens of the beautiful city
> are terrified. How can one blame them? Bombs
> come out of nowhere and at random times. I feel
> sure the Germans are using Big Bertha for that
> very reason—to further destroy the morale of the
> Parisians who have already suffered so very much.
> Our planes have searched in vain for the source of
> the shelling, but it is well hidden.

A few weeks later, Carl read of the nightmarish blow that hit Paris on Good Friday, March 29. A shell from Big Bertha struck the Church of St. Gervais, killing and wounding many worshipers, including several American soldiers.

The incident filled many Americans at home with even more hatred. Their hatred led to more acts of violence. A German-American man named Robert Prager was lynched. Prager's death made the headlines the morning of April 6. Carl could hardly get his papers folded for trying to read the article.

Mr. Prager was from Dresden, Germany, and wasn't a citizen, but from what the article said, he wanted to be. The mineworker had even attempted to become a union member, but his membership had been refused. Prager had been singled out by a mob and accused of being a spy and a traitor. They took him outside the small town of Collinsville, Illinois, and strung him from a tree.

The poor man evidently didn't have someone like Dr. Richard Allerton to come to his defense. It made Carl even more thankful that Papa hadn't been hurt when he was arrested.

Carl's favorite place in all of Central High School was the library. He spent most of his study hall times scouring the shelves for books he'd not yet read.

As spring approached, bigger and bigger gaps appeared in the library shelves. It took a while before Carl realized exactly what was happening. When it finally dawned on him, he was stunned. Books were being removed that were about Germany, were written by German authors, or were German language textbooks.

He argued with himself at first—because it was just too impossible to believe. But the awful truth hit home one day when the students were called into an assembly. There in the large high school auditorium, they were instructed about the books.

"This will be your opportunity to do your bit for the war cause," the principal, Mr. Thompson, told the students. The short paunchy principal, with his thin gray hair parted precisely in the middle and slicked down on both sides, was always attired in meticulously pressed gray suits. His dark-rimmed glasses added to his studious appearance. Directly behind him, the crimson stage curtains glided open to reveal stacks and stacks of books.

"Each student," he told them, "will come up and take a book. We will then file outside, where each one of you may take part in throwing this dangerous literature into trash bins. They will then be taken to be burned."

Instantly Carl's mind flashed back to the news articles that came out of Belgium three years ago when the war first began. The Germans, marching through the tiny country of Belgium, had torched the ancient libraries of Louvain. Americans everywhere were outraged over the incident. His stomach churned as he wondered how this burning could be any different.

Across the aisle and down a row from Carl sat Jillian Oliver. Unexpectedly she turned around and looked at him with large, sad, brown eyes. Something told Carl she didn't at all agree with what was happening.

Woodenly Carl moved along, pushed and shoved by the crowds of students, none of whom seemed to be aware of just how serious this was. If every student would rise up in revolt, maybe this thing would stop. After all, the school officials couldn't expel everyone. But no one spoke.

Out on the school grounds, empty boxes, barrels, and trash cans waited. Why, Carl wondered, didn't they just cart the books off instead of having the students participate? How strange it all seemed.

After Jillian had dropped her book into a trash bin, she slipped back past Carl and softly whispered, "This is ludicrous."

Carl looked up to see Sidney glaring at him with hate burning in his eyes. Weldon, as usual, was close by his side.

Carl didn't dare look at the book in his hands. Not until

it dropped into the basket did he glance at the title. It was a simple German language textbook. What harm could it possibly cause?

Suddenly there was a noise behind him. A fellow freshman—and fellow German American—Franz Baergen stood with his book clutched to his chest, not moving. He was holding up the entire line. Some of the other students began to yell at him to throw the book in. He refused to move.

After a moment, Mr. Whitney, the math instructor, came up. "What seems to be the matter?" he asked.

"He won't throw his book in," someone yelled. "The Hun is loyal to the Kaiser and won't do his part."

Mr. Whitney glared at Franz. "Why won't you throw the book in, Franz?" he asked.

"These books have nothing to do with the war," the boy stated in a clear voice, loud enough for everyone around him to hear. "If these books never left the library shelves, it would not make one iota of difference in the fighting in Europe."

The other students began to boo and jeer. Then Mr. Thompson was sent for. Within minutes the portly man, carrying his natty snap-brimmed hat, strode up to the scene.

"What's happening here?" he demanded. "What's the meaning of this delay?"

"This boy refuses to cooperate," Mr. Whitney said.

"Is this true?" Mr. Thompson asked.

Franz looked the principal square in the eye and repeated what he'd said before. The removal of these books had no bearing on the war in Europe.

Carl had never seen Mr. Thompson so enraged. The man's face grew crimson.

"You there!" Mr. Thompson pointed randomly into the

crowd at Weldon Pritchard. "Take the book from this boy and show him what's to be done with enemy propaganda."

"My pleasure, sir!" Weldon stomped forward. Towering over the small freshman, he literally ripped the book from his hands and threw it as hard as he could into a metal trash barrel. It landed with a sickening crashing sound.

"Thank you, young man," Mr. Thompson said. Turning to Franz, he said, "You come to the office with me."

As Franz walked away, he yelled out, "It's a travesty!" at the top of his voice.

The words echoed in Carl's head for days. How wonderful Franz must have felt at having been able to express himself so freely. So courageously.

However, two days later Carl caught sight of Franz in the school hallway. His eyes were swollen almost completely shut, his lip was cut, and there was a nasty gash on one cheek. It didn't take any brilliance for Carl to figure out what had happened. Franz had been beaten up by one or more of the other students.

How Carl wished he'd taken a stand along with Franz. Perhaps if two of them had stood together, others might have joined them. At any rate, between the two of them, they might have put up a pretty good fight.

CHAPTER 9
Farm Worker

Larry was extremely proud of his pictures of the first American Pursuit Squadron, the 94th Squadron, which hung on the wall of the upstairs playroom at the Allerton house. These fighter pilots flew the fast SPAD fighters, and their symbol was a picture of Uncle Sam's hat with a red ring around it. They called themselves "The-Hat-in-the-Ring Squadron."

"They shoot German planes right out of the skies," Larry told Carl. He'd dragged Carl into the family playroom to show the pictures he'd clipped from newspapers and magazines.

"This," he said pointing to the newest picture, "is Captain Eddie Rickenbacker. He's my hero, that's for sure. I want to be just like him."

Carl leaned close to read the headlines: *Rickenbacker Downs Foe. Former Automobile Racer, Now Airman, Fights Three Germans—With the American Army in France, May 17.*

Since Carl read the papers daily, he already knew most of this information, but Larry's fascination with planes was almost as strong as Carl's fascination with photography, so he let him talk. Sometimes they discussed the importance of photography in the war. Brave pilots photographed enemy lines, flying deep into enemy territory on these missions.

"And this one," Larry said, pointing to yet another magazine clipping, "is what the Germans call the 'Flying Circus,' because the planes are all painted in bright colors. The commander of the squadron is known as the Red Baron, but his real name is Baron Manfred von Richthofen."

From off the floor, Larry picked up one of his toy airplanes. "The Red Baron is the scourge of the skies. But one of these days his luck will run out, and one of our Yanks— maybe Eddie Rickenbacker—will shoot him down out of the skies!!"

With that he dropped the toy plane, allowing it to clatter to the floor. "Death to the Red Baron," he croaked in a dramatic manner.

Not enjoying the talk of death and dying, Carl was pleased when they were called downstairs to join the adults in making a batch of ice cream. The boys were needed to take turns turning the crank on the freezer.

They were gathered in the backyard, and Carl was taking his turn at cranking when Aunt Frances approached him.

"Carl," she said, "remember when I told you that Clara Ueland was appointed head of the Food Production and Conservation Committee for the state of Minnesota?"

"Yes, ma'am," Carl answered, pushing the crank. It was getting tighter and tighter.

"Well, the committee is facing a big problem. With all our young farmers going off to war, there aren't enough workers on the farms around our state. The committee is looking for student-aged boys to board and work on the farms."

Carl stopped cranking and stared at her. "Work on a farm?"

Aunt Frances nodded. "That's what I said." Pointing to the freezer she said, "You'd better keep turning that crank, or it'll freeze, and you'll never get it turned."

"Oh, yes. I'm sorry."

"I wondered if you might like to be one of the boys to volunteer."

Her words seemed almost too good to be true. To get out of the city and live on a farm. To get away from all the prejudice and harassment. Enjoy the wide open spaces. "I'd like that very much. When will all this happen?"

"The biggest need will be during haying time and wheat harvest. But some farmers are asking for boys to come right now. Of course, you'd have to finish out the school year. . ."

"If this is a special war effort like you say, maybe I could take my final tests early and be excused." Carl pushed the crank one more time. "I think it's ready." He lifted the lid for Aunt Frances to take a look.

"It's ready!" Before everyone came swarming with dishes

in hand, she said softly, "I'll talk to your parents and see what we can do."

On April 21, just a few days after that visit, Larry's prediction came true. The Red Baron was indeed shot down by an American fighter pilot. The baron had downed eighty Allied planes before his killing was brought to a fiery end.

Carl thought of his cousin Larry when he read about the Red Baron in the paper, but other matters were holding his attention. Would his parents agree to his leaving school early and working in the country? Many decisions seemed to hinge on whether or not something was related to the "war effort." Carl's leaving Minneapolis was treated the same way. Aunt Frances spoke with his parents, and they readily agreed.

Farmers who needed boys right away filed applications with the committee. From there, Clara Ueland and her staff worked with the schools to find possible candidates. In Carl's case, because Aunt Frances was such a good friend of Mrs. Ueland, the contact was made directly rather than going through the school. Mrs. Ueland, herself, made the phone call to the school office to make sure Carl could take his tests early and leave town as soon as possible.

Details fell into place so quickly, Carl could barely grasp what was happening. He was too excited to think how scared he was. He'd never been away from home for even one night. None of his family ever traveled, so they didn't have anything in which Carl could pack his belongings. When they learned of the situation, Uncle Erik and Aunt Esther loaned Carl their valise.

Within a week after he'd spoken to Aunt Frances, Carl learned he would be staying with the Mowry family on a farm outside of Spencerville. The town was almost fifty miles from Minneapolis. The Mowrys, he was told, had two sons in the army and three children at home.

"Who's going to tend the garden while Carl's gone?" Edie asked at supper. It was the night before Carl was to leave.

"That'll be your job now," Carl teased.

Edie let out an audible groan that made them all laugh.

The garden was already full of early vegetables in this the second year of the war. Carl was proud of how he'd learned to "winter over" the plot with mulch and compost. He'd planted potatoes and English peas in early March, as soon as the ground was thawed out enough to till.

"The gardening will be taken over by the whole family," Papa said. "We'll all go out in the evenings and work on it together."

"Which means," Mama said softly, "that it takes five of us to replace our Carl."

Her compliment made Carl blush. He knew Mama hated to see him leave.

After supper there was another letter from Truman to read aloud. Every time a letter arrived, Carl heaved a silent sigh of relief. Many of the stars on the service flags hanging in parlor windows were now gold, which meant a son had been slain on the battlefield. Carl never saw one without thinking of Truman and praying for his safe return.

Recent news from France told of the heroic efforts of the U.S. troops at Chateau-Thierry. They had taken a stand in an area the French had abandoned as lost. The Germans had been marching toward Paris—the first forward movement of the war in many months—and they expected little resistance. But they hadn't reckoned on the fierce determination of the fighting Yanks. At least that's what Truman's letter told them.

A division of American troops dynamited the bridge that led across the Marne River, slowing the German advance. This daring venture cut off the Americans' own route of escape, but they managed to escape during the night with heavy casualties.

Truman's letter read:

> *Attacking is a good deal different than sitting in a trench. A barrage began first to prepare the way for us. A few minutes after the barrage started, someone shouted, "Let's at them!" And over the top we went. The barrage had cleared the way so there wasn't much opposition, but I threw my grenades in a bay and got a couple hits. We ran for a ways, then slid into another trench. Trenches are everywhere.*
>
> *Strange as it may seem, my heart is hardened to the sight of the dead enemy. I'm told that fields farther ahead of us are covered with dead Huns. When I see our boys around me dying daily, it increases my desire to deal out misery to the enemy.*

These parts of Truman's letters bothered Carl the most. He wondered if the same Truman would ever come home again. He tried to hear Truman's voice as Tim read the letter, but it seemed like nothing more than a newspaper article. When Truman began writing about the food, it was somewhat easier to read.

> *Our breakfast is hardtack crackers, bacon, and coffee. Sometimes mush made from cornmeal. They*

*fry tinned salmon, which we call "goldfish," and
the beef stew is called "slumgullion." The corned
beef is the worst. The stringy stuff we call "monkey
meat." Who knows whether or not monkey meat
would be any worse?*

*To while away the hours in the trenches, we
have target practice shooting at the rats. Some are
as big as a small dog. What a feast we have spread
for them out across this vast countryside. I wonder
what they ate before we arrived?*

*To a man, we are grateful for the passing of
winter. But I can truthfully say it's been this winter
that made us tough. The Yanks are now an incredible force to be reckoned with!*

Once the letter was read, Papa put on his gold-rimmed
glasses and read from the Bible as he did every night. Carl
still had not fully taken in the fact that the next night he
would not be there in the parlor with them. Once the
Scriptures were read, Papa prayed. He especially prayed for
Carl to be kept safe and for the Lord to use him as a witness
of His love and mercy. Carl wasn't sure about that last part.
He hoped Papa wasn't expecting too much of him.

Mama and Papa and Tim had to go to work the next morning. But Mama called the schools and had Edie and Lydia
excused for the first hour. Uncle Richard was coming over
in his Hupmobile to take Carl to the train station, then take
the girls on to school.

Before they left the house, Mama and Papa said good-
bye to Carl. Both of them kissed him and hugged him.
Mama cautioned him to live as an example of what he'd

been taught at home.

"I will, Mama," he said past the lump in his throat. "I promise."

Papa said, "I'm proud of you, Carl. I'll always be proud of you."

"Thank you, Papa," he answered in a cracked voice.

Even Frosty was repeatedly rubbing against his legs as though he, too, knew that Carl was leaving.

Uncle Richard was jovial and kind as he stood with the three Schmidts on the platform waiting for the "all aboard" to be sounded. "Don't come home with any hayseed in your hair," he teased. But when it came time to say good-bye, he shook Carl's hand firmly, looked him in the eyes, and said, "We're proud of you, Carlton, for doing your part."

Lydia and Edie were both in tears, which made it doubly hard for Carl to fight back his own tears. He boarded the train and flung himself into a seat by the window. He placed his lunch sack in his lap and tucked his valise firmly between his feet. His camera and film were in that valise, and he planned to watch it with an eagle eye.

Suddenly the train lurched forward. The whistle pierced the air. Carl's heart was in his mouth as he waved one last time to the girls and Uncle Richard. Edie's face was so sad Carl thought he couldn't stand it. That's when his own tears escaped. He pulled out his handkerchief and kept his face turned toward the window. Perhaps no one would notice.

CHAPTER 10

On the Farm

Carl's nervous stomach wouldn't allow him to eat much of the lunch Edie packed for him. For the most part, he stared in awe at how fast the scenery flew past his window and reveled in the rocking sensation of the train car and the bumping and clacking of the wheels on the track.

The farther they traveled west, the more farms spread out across the countryside and the fewer forests blocked the view. While it wasn't exactly like the scenes of the Wild West in the flickers, at least there were no crowded streets or tall buildings.

As the miles whipped by, Carl thought about meeting his host family for the first time. Aunt Frances said this man had two boys over in France. Perhaps Carl should simply introduce himself as Carlton *Smith*. Everything would be so much easier. So much simpler. No one need ever know he was part German.

The thought tumbled around in his mind for a time, like Frosty playing with a ball of yarn. Then he thought of Papa being put in jail for something he didn't do. Papa would never change his name just to avoid problems, any more than he would stop working with the union in order to avoid problems.

By the time the conductor called out, "Next stop, Spencerville!" Carl knew he could never deny the name Papa had given to him, no matter what the cost.

Carl grabbed up his valise and gazed at the tiny station as metal screeched against metal and the train huffed to a stop. Spencerville was barely a wide spot in the road. If he were not getting off, Carl wondered if the train would have stopped at all.

As he stepped down onto the platform, he looked around, but no one was there. A few yards from the station was the Spencerville Hotel, which was only two stories tall. There was also a livery, a blacksmith shop, a general store, and a few other shops. Not much. Not much at all.

Carl stood for a time as the train's piercing whistle gave off its shrill warning. The train hissed a cloud of steam as it gathered momentum and gradually pulled away from the station. Unsure of what to do, Carl went inside the station and stepped up to the station master. "Excuse me."

The gray-haired man adjusted the glasses on his nose. "Hey there, sonny. What can I do for you?"

"I'm looking for the Mowry family. Have they been here?"

"Ah yes, you're the city boy what's come to lend a hand." The man stood up from his swivel chair and looked over the counter to fully inspect the boy before him. "Horace is gonna be surely disappointed they didn't send one no bigger than you."

Carl felt himself stiffen. He wasn't exactly small for his age. And no one had said he was supposed to be a certain size. "Has he been here?"

"They're down at the general store fetching supplies. They'll be along shortly. Just take yourself a seat." He waved toward the wooden benches and went back to work.

In a matter of minutes, a wagon drawn by two magnificent roans with inky-black manes and tails pulled up to the station. Three children piled out of the back—two boys and a younger girl—before the father had time to pull on the brake.

The man stepped heavily down to the ground and wrapped the reins to the hitching rail. He made no move to help his wife down, but she gathered up the skirt of her simple cotton dress and stepped down as though she always took care of herself. Her cotton sunbonnet looked terribly old-fashioned. Carl hurried out of the station to meet them.

Mr. Mowry was a thick, rough-looking man with steely eyes peering from under thick craggy eyebrows. He obviously cared very little about personal appearance. His flannel shirt and loose-fitting trousers were soiled, and his suspenders looked as though he'd worn them forever. He didn't bother to pull off his old felt hat with the sweat-stained band. He looked down at Carl and said, "What's your name, boy?"

The two boys were standing close by, staring at Carl as though he were a strange specimen they'd never seen before. The little girl hid behind her mama's skirts. Her dress was as faded and patched as her mother's, and her limp sunbonnet had seen better days. Carl wondered what Edie would think if she had to wear such a getup.

"My name's Carl Schmidt," Carl said politely, stretching out his hand. "And you're Mr. Mowry?"

The outstretched hand was ignored. "Schmidt? *Schmidt?* Now ain't that a fine kettle of fish. I send two strapping boys off to fight Krauts, and what do I get? A Kraut to come and live on my property and eat at my table." His voice fairly roared. The two boys giggled and elbowed one another.

"Never mind, Horace," his wife said in a hushed tone. "We got no choice. The work has to be done."

"Mebbe so," he said, turning on his heel and heading back toward the wagon, "but I don't have to like it. Or him!"

Carl's dream of escaping from prejudice was quickly deflated. He picked up his valise and started to follow when Mrs. Mowry came up to him. "Horace is upset on account of Arthur and Foster leaving. It just ain't been the same with them gone."

She reached down and touched the little girl. "This here's Dora. She just turned seven." Pointing to the older boy who was following his father, she said, "That there is Elmer. He's ten, and Chester here is eight." The younger boy looked at Carl, wrinkled up his nose, and stuck out his tongue.

"Now, Chester," his mother said in a weary tone, "that's no way to act."

"Shake a leg there," Mr. Mowry called out from up on the wagon seat. "Chores gotta be done afore dark."

Carl climbed up into the back of the wagon with the

three Mowry children and the farm supplies. Dora stared at him with wide eyes while the boys smirked and made faces. Carl felt he was being pummeled senseless as the wagon bounced along the country road.

At one point a farm truck came rumbling out of the distance toward them in a cloud of dust. As the driver approached, he smiled and waved, but the surly Mr. Mowry didn't move a muscle.

"Proudful old buzzard," he muttered after the truck had passed. "Thinks he's better than anybody in the county just cuz he's got him some silly machinery. I pulled him out of the mud last spring."

None of the family members said a word in response. Carl wondered what Mr. Mowry would think of all the automobiles traveling about the streets of Minneapolis.

The Mowry farm was the standard hundred acres, with a house and barn and various smaller outbuildings. The structures could have used a little paint and fixing up but appeared to be firm and sturdy. Mr. Mowry seemed to be a person who cared little about finishing touches. Carl was to bed down in a room at the back of the barn, which was fine with him.

Mr. Mowry drove the team up to the big barn and hollered, "Whoa there." When the wagon came to a stop, Mrs. Mowry helped herself down and took Dora and went toward the house without a word. When they were almost to the house, a gray and white kitten bounded off the porch and almost leaped into Dora's arms. The sight of the little girl cuddling the kitten gave Carl a pang of homesickness for Edie.

Elmer and Chester set about taking the harnesses off the horses. As Carl watched and listened, he learned their names were Streak and Lightning. He'd never seen such beautiful animals. Not even the horse he'd ridden at the Uelands' place could match these for sleekness and beauty.

After the boys had brushed the horses down, they turned the steeds out into a paddock behind the barn. Two more horses stood in the paddock, but they were giant workhorses. They were at least part Clydesdale. Powerful-looking fellows. How Carl hoped he'd have a chance to work with them. Sometime later, he learned their names were Clyde and Dale. Fitting, but not too original. If they were Carl's, he would have named them something like Thor and Goliath.

Mr. Mowry told the boys to show Carl his room then get to their chores. Jabbing a thumb at Carl, he added, "And show the Kraut what's to be done. I'm going out to check on Mack."

After their father was out of earshot, Chester said, "Mack's our mean, mad bull. You gotta watch out for him."

"Yeah," Elmer echoed. "He gored a hired man of ours once. Almost all his guts fell out."

"Oooeee!" Chester made a terrible face. "It was somethin' awful to behold."

Carl listened and attempted to measure whether they were being truthful or not. He'd heard that bulls were mean. He studied the two Mowry boys as they led him around to the back of the barn and showed him his room.

Elmer and Chester were like two peas in a pod. The only difference was that Elmer was a smidgen taller and his ears stuck out like the car doors on Uncle Richard's Hupmobile. Chester was a bit smaller with a face full of freckles. Both boys wore overalls and ran barefooted, with frayed straw hats on their heads.

When Elmer opened the door to the room, Carl wasn't

sure what to expect. He was surprised to see a small, neatly swept room with an old bureau, a table and chair, and a cot covered with a thin cotton mattress. The cot had been made up with clean sheets and a faded quilt. The double-hung window looked to be in fair shape with only one cracked pane. Possibly the room at one time had housed a hired hand. The one who'd been gored by the mad bull perhaps?

Once Carl had stowed his belongings in his room, the three boys headed out to the pasture to bring in the cows. As soon as they were out of sight of the house and barn, Chester screamed, "Look out! Snake! Snake!"

Carl must have jumped straight up into the air. "Where? Where?" he cried, his heart pounding. It took only a moment before he realized he'd been had. The two brothers were convulsing in fits of giggles—just short of rolling on the ground. From then on, Carl was onto them. He'd have to keep an eye out. They were definitely mischief bound.

Once the cows were rounded up, brought to the barn, and put in their stanchions, it was time to teach Carl how to milk. Carl was embarrassed and awkward at his first attempts. Of course he was getting no help from the boys, who simply told him to grab hold and pull. When he did, the old cow's back leg came flying forward. The little stool he was sitting on wasn't any too substantial to begin with, and the flying leg sent Carl sprawling on his back. By now the boys were in hysterics. Mr. Mowry chose that moment to step inside the barn.

"This ain't no time to be fooling around," he said. "Get the work done, or I'll take a razor strop to the whole lot of you."

Narrowing his steely eyes, he fixed a steady gaze on Carl. "Don't suppose you ever laid eyes on a cow before.

Elmer, don't just stand there. Show him how to milk. I don't see how having a mindless city slicker here is gonna help me one iota!"

Elmer grabbed the upset stool and began to milk the cow, who now stood still as a statue, except for gently switching her tail. Carl watched closely and could see Elmer's hands started at the top of the teat and worked easily downward. He was sure he could learn it.

The hog pen was a solid stone structure that stood about chest-high to Carl. It was a good thing it was solid. If he had any doubts about the meanness of Mack the bull, Carl had no doubts about these huge pigs. They'd as soon eat the hand that fed them as the feed itself.

Once the cows were fed and milked, the horses fed, the pigs fed, the chickens fed, the eggs gathered, and about a dozen other things, it was finally time for supper. Since Carl was to sleep in the barn, he wasn't sure whether or not he was to eat out there as well. But the dour Mr. Mowry waved him toward the house and told him to wash up at the granite basin on a stump by the back door.

A dirty towel hung on a wire beside the basin. Carl decided to let the air dry his hands. Before going inside, both Mowry boys picked up an armload of wood from the woodpile for their mama's cookstove.

Supper was strained. The children seemed frightened to speak in their father's presence. Even Mrs. Mowry spoke in hushed tones. There was pork for supper. Carl soon learned there was often pork for supper, and pork for breakfast as well. And fried potatoes swimming in pork grease. They drank mugs of stout coffee with no cream or sugar. At home, only Papa took coffee. The platter of red radishes and green onions in the center of the table was the only touch of color to liven up the plain fare.

Carl wondered what Mr. Herbert Hoover would have thought if he could have seen their table. The Mowrys acted as though they'd never heard of the meatless, porkless, wheatless days.

No one thanked the Lord for the meal. They just dove in. Carl silently said his thanks.

They had barely started eating, when Mr. Mowry started ranting about a clan of Mennonites who lived in the area. "A particular type and kind of Hun," he said, his gruff voice raised for emphasis. "Refuse to put on a uniform like my two boys done. Think they're too good, I suppose."

After he warmed up to his subject, he showed he could go on about it nonstop. When he finished his meal, Mr. Mowry slurped his coffee and leaned back in his chair. Summing up his views of the Mennonites, he said, "Spies paid by the Kaiser, no doubt, the whole blessed lot of 'em."

Carl wasn't sure if Mr. Mowry talked like this at every meal, or if the man was trying to send him a message. Either way, it was extremely uncomfortable. Any mention of the word *spy* made Carl think of Papa's gruesome experience. As soon as he could, he excused himself and went to his room, where he could be alone.

Not a bit sleepy, Carl crawled up into the haymow and sat looking out across the miles of pastures and farmland. As the sun was setting and turning everything soft and rosy, he took a few photographs. It was almost dark when he climbed down and went to his room. Thankfully, there was a latch on the door. That should keep out a couple little pranksters.

Stripping to his underwear, Carl slid between the clean sheets. He was tense as a board, listening to the millions of unfamiliar sounds. The horses stamping and snorting in the corral, the chickens roosting in the rafters of the barn, the barn kittens playing up in the haymow.

Suddenly something cool, clammy, and wet touched his bare foot. Like a coiled spring suddenly released, Carl flew out of bed, stubbing his toe and almost knocking over the nearby chair in the process. In the dim moonlight that spilled through the window, he could barely make out the form of the bed. Picking up his shoe, he cautiously drew back the covers. A fat green frog stared at him with glassy eyes. In a flash, Carl unlatched the door, grabbed the frog by one leg, and heaved him as far and as hard as he could.

Those Mowry boys would bear watching. More so than he'd previously thought.

CHAPTER 11
Saving Fancy

The Mowry family rose long before the sun came up. At breakfast the two boys asked Carl how he'd slept. By the way they were grinning, there was no doubt the frog had been their doing. He told them he'd slept like a baby. Truth was, he'd hardly slept a wink.

Carl soon became thankful for the hours he'd spent hoeing his garden in the city. Those toned muscles came in handy as he carried five-gallon buckets of feed and water to the animals and then slopped the hogs. Never in his life had he ever smelled anything so rank as that hog pen. And the flies were thick. Looking at those fat old hogs wallowing in the mud and grunting and rutting around made the fried pork he'd eaten for breakfast sit like lead in his stomach.

Each day Mr. Mowry hitched up Clyde and Dale to some farm implement and went out to the fields. Carl had hoped he could work with those magnificent horses, but he was told to hoe the garden, which was about four times as large as the one in the Schmidts' backyard.

There were half a dozen long rows of sweet corn, whose glossy green stalks stood about a foot tall, all of which needed to be weeded. Then there were the rows of tomatoes, beans, and other vegetables.

The boys, on the other hand, went to the fields with their papa. Carl resigned himself to the fact that Mr. Mowry probably wouldn't trust him with any more than hoeing the garden. But at least the boys weren't around to pester him.

At midmorning, Dora came out carrying water to Carl in a Mason jar. Shyly she handed it to him. In her other arm was the gray and white kitten he'd seen her pick up the day before.

"What's your kitten's name?"

"Fancy."

"That's an interesting name. Does it mean something?"

She rubbed one bare foot on top of the other. "I have a hankering for fancy things, but Papa says I don't need none." Kissing the top of the kitten's head, she added, "This is my only fancy thing."

Carl thought about Edie and how she loved pretty dresses. Even though they didn't have a lot of money, Mama and Papa—and Lydia as well—did what they could to give Edie a few pretty things. He decided to change the subject. "How did you tame this one? All the kittens I saw in the barn are wild as can be."

She shrugged her thin little shoulders. "I don't know. We just loved each other right off. She never runned away."

Carl nodded and handed her back the empty jar. God must have known this lonely little girl needed a friend, he thought as he watched her tripping back into the house. As he finished one row and started up the next, Carl thought about the two older Mowry sons who'd joined the army. As harsh and severe as their papa was, he didn't wonder that they'd jumped at the chance to get away. Perhaps they thought a war would be easier.

After the noon meal, Mr. Mowry showed Carl how to shovel manure from the corral into the manure spreader. Carl hadn't even known there was such a thing as a manure spreader. For his little garden, he'd just shoveled from his wheelbarrow onto the garden area. But of course you couldn't do that with acres and acres of crops.

The spreader was parked just the other side of the corral. It was no small task to scoop up the mix of mud, manure, and old rotted hay, and sling it into the spreader. But Carl put himself into it and didn't shirk. By the time the summer was over, he'd be a regular Paul Bunyan.

Carl thought that Elmer and Chester had gone back to the field with their papa, so when he heard a voice from the other end of the corral, he spun around in surprise.

There were the boys, hanging on the gate, both grinning like Cheshire cats. "Look out!" Elmer hollered. "It's Mack, the mad bull!"

Sure enough, they'd opened a gate from the pasture. The massive bull was sauntering into the corral toward him. That old bull's head must have been a foot across from horn to horn. Carl's heart stopped, and his legs refused to move. Slowly the bull was coming closer, his head down. Carl wondered what his family would say when they learned what had happened to him—gored to death by a mad bull.

"Run, Carl Schmidt!" Chester shouted. "Run for your life!"

The words seemed to shake Carl loose. He threw down his shovel and turned to run, but his boot was stuck in the slimy mud of the corral. Now his heart was pounding so hard it was thudding in his ears. Reaching down to pull the boot loose, he then ran toward the wooden fence and started to jump up on it, but his wet boots slipped, and he fell into the mud. And the bull kept coming.

Carl closed his eyes, waiting for death to come and carry him away. Nothing happened. But he could hear the snickers. When he opened his eyes, the bull had sauntered right past him to the feed trough. He'd been had again!

The two ornery boys were doubled over with laughter. "Mad bull, mad bull," Elmer taunted. "Old Mack is more like a pussycat."

"We raised him from a little baby calf," Chester added.

Carl got to his feet, picked up his shovel, and went back to work, pretending it had never happened. Later, after the other boys left to go back to the field, Carl thought about what had happened. Their tricks were really quite harmless, and they probably hadn't had much to laugh about for a very long time. Sooner or later, they'd run out of ideas. He'd just have to endure their teasing until they did.

The days blended into a routine of sorts. Carl did exactly what Mr. Mowry told him to do. Soon he was taught how to harness and unharness the workhorses. Lifting the huge soft leather collars up over their necks was quite a feat. Carl petted them and talked to them and slipped them carrots from the garden as often as he could. Sometimes he'd go to the corral after dark and talk to them. Eventually, all four came to him at the sound of his voice.

Carl checked his bed thoroughly every night before retiring, but by the second week, he was so exhausted, he could have slept with a dozen frogs in the bed. In spite of the surly Mr. Mowry, Carl loved the country. The clean air, the animals, the wide expanses of blue skies. In the city you could never see so much sky at one time. The cloud formations, the sunrises, the sunsets all fascinated him.

At night he could see millions of stars like pinpricks in a velvet blanket. An awesome sight. Whenever he was alone, he brought out his camera and took photographs. Tim had promised to develop all the film he would send home. But he wasn't sure yet when and how he would do the mailing.

One evening, however, Mr. Mowry told Carl he was to take the wagon into town the next day to take a broken plowshare to the blacksmith for repairs. Now he'd have the opportunity to go to the post office. Both Elmer and Chester begged to be able to go with Carl, but Mr. Mowry said there was too much work to do for three hands to be off doing nothing. Carl felt badly for them. He was sure Elmer could hitch up Lightning and Streak and take the wagon to town just as well as Carl could.

When supper was finished, Carl went up into the haymow to sit in the hay and write letters, one to the family and, of course, one to Truman. Just as he started on his second letter, he heard a terrible ruckus in the barnyard below. Carl laid aside his paper and pen and crawled across the hay to the window to take a look. The boys were teasing Dora by taking her kitten.

The tricks Elmer and Chester had played on Carl had been harmless, but this got his dander up something fierce. He leaped back over the piles of hay to the ladder and scurried down. As he came through the front of the barn, the boys were laughing, Dora was screaming, and the kitten was yowling.

"Let her kitten go!" Carl ordered.

His voice startled them, which gave the kitten the opportunity to bare her claws and leap from Elmer's hands.

The boys ignored Carl and started chasing the terrified kitten. "Get her!" Elmer yelled at Chester. "Get that cat!"

The kitten was making a beeline for the hog pen. Carl's breath caught in his throat. He'd seen those fat hogs move. They may look fat and slow, but they could grab that kitten and have it gone in a flash.

"No, no, Fancy!" Dora screamed. "Not the hog pen!"

Carl raced past the boys, and with an agile leap, he was up on the rock wall, looking down on the terrified kitten sitting in the mud in the corner of the pen. He ran around the top of the wall to where the kitten was, jumped down, and scooped the kitten up just as four big hogs came racing toward him. He yanked out his shirttail, rolled the kitten up in it, and heaved himself up on the wall just as the grunting, snorting swine reached him.

Gasping for air, Carl dropped to the ground, sunk to his knees in the dirt, and cradled the warm, quivering kitten against his chest. Fancy must have had sense enough to know she'd been rescued. She didn't bare a claw.

Carl turned back the edge of his shirttail to look at Fancy's little face. "It's all right, Fancy," he cooed to her. "You're safe now."

Carl looked up to see a tear-stained face smiling at him. "You saved my kitty. You saved my Fancy."

"I never seen nothing like that in all my born days," Chester said, his eyes wide.

"You jumped right in there with them old hogs," Elmer said, not bothering to disguise his awe. "I wouldn't never do such a thing. Not even Arthur woulda done that."

Carl motioned to Dora to sit in the dirt beside him. When she did, he gently transferred the kitten from his shirt over into her skirt. The kitten was still quivering but gave a tiny mew. Dora wiped at the muddy cat with the hem of her dress, loving and petting her.

"Now," Carl said to the boys. "What say you find a different toy and leave Dora's kitten alone. All right?"

"Yeah," Elmer said, his eyes still wide with wonder. "All right. I mean, we will. Won't we, Chester?"

"Yeah," came the reply.

Carl stood to his feet and brushed the dirt off his trousers. "If you don't mind, I'll get back to what I was doing."

Dora wiped at her wet cheeks with a dirty hand, making the smears even worse. "Thank you, Carl. Thank you for saving Fancy."

"My pleasure."

Once Carl was back up in the haymow with his letters, he started shaking from head to toe. He could hardly believe he'd actually put himself right in the path of those wretched hogs just to save a little kitten. But he'd done it. And for once in his life, he had not run away.

In the process, he'd made a powerful impression on two ornery little boys.

CHAPTER 12
Mennonites

The next morning, Mrs. Mowry gave Carl a list of things to purchase at the general store while the plow was being fixed. Mr. Mowry was out in the east section fixing fences.

"Streak and Lightning know the way to town and back," Elmer said as he helped Carl hitch the team up to the farm wagon. "Won't be no trouble at all."

As Carl pulled himself up into the hard wooden seat, he said, "If I had my way, I'd take the two of you along."

"You would?" Chester asked.

"I would." Carl shook the reins. "See you this afternoon."

Mrs. Mowry was on the porch with Dora by her side. She shaded her eyes with her hand and waved good-bye to Carl. Dora clutched Fancy with one hand and waved with the other.

Carl thought about the strange Mowry family as the horses loped along, raising little puffs of dust with each clop of their hooves. Carl's own papa might be ostracized for being a union man and for being German, but Carl would take Papa over grumpy old Horace Mowry any day of the week.

In town, Carl purchased a Minneapolis newspaper and a new book to read, using his own money. There were no newspapers at the Mowry farm and certainly no newsreels to watch. He had no idea how the war was going.

He also purchased three pieces of stick candy and had the grocer put them in a paper bag to take to the Mowry children. At the post office, he mailed off his film to Tim and his letters. In the Mowry's mail was a letter to Carl from the family but nothing from Truman.

Since the plow still was not ready, he strolled down the sidewalk and looked around. It seemed as though he'd been tucked away in hiding for years rather than for one month. At the end of Main Street stood a small stone church. Looking at the church, he suddenly realized that he very much missed being in a church service every Sunday morning. Mama had made sure he brought along his small New Testament, but he hadn't spent much time reading it.

As he turned to go up the other side of the street, he was startled to hear voices—voices speaking in German. It had been a long time since he'd heard German being spoken openly. Beside the church sat two youngsters, a boy who looked to be Carl's age or just older and a younger girl.

They were eating lunch from a basket. The girl wore a plain gray dress with no lace or ruffles, and the boy was dressed all in black with no buttons on his shirt. Carl knew immediately they were Mennonites.

They evidently had not noticed Carl. The boy was trying to shush the girl. "Try to talk only English in town, Leota," the boy was saying. "Remember what Papa told to us."

Carl started to walk on but then stopped. Something urged him to leave the sidewalk and walk over to them. "Hello," he said, tipping his cap.

The boy jumped to his feet; fear was written in his eyes. "Leota, she iss sorry to speak der German. She just forgets. You won't tell on her, will you?"

Carl smiled. "My name is Carl Schmidt. I'm staying with the Mowry family to help on the farm." He reached out his hand.

The boy smiled and relaxed. "You are German?" he asked returning the handshake.

"My papa's name is Hans Schmidt."

The boy nodded. "We are Helmut and Leota Kordzik."

Leota arose and gave a little curtsy.

Carl nodded to her. "I didn't mean to interrupt your lunch."

"Just finished, we were." Helmut spread his wide farm-boy hands. "Sorry, not even a crumb to offer you."

"I'm fine," Carl told him. "Mrs. Mowry sent a couple biscuits and sausage along with me."

"Mr. Mowry, he is all right to you?" Leota asked softly.

"Leota," Helmut scolded. "That is none of our business."

"Mr. Mowry tolerates me."

"He is not a kind man," Leota said.

"It iss true. But then," Helmut added, "even those who

used to be kind to us are kind no more. Those who we thought were trusted and beloved neighbors can no longer be trusted."

"What do you mean?" Carl asked.

Helmut waved to the shady spot under the oak. "Come, sit down."

Carl sat down with them and for a few minutes listened as they told of the threats of violence that spread through the countryside daily because Mennonite young men refused to go to war and because Mennonites everywhere spoke out against the war.

"For hundreds of years, our people have held to the belief that it is against God's Word to bear arms against a fellow human being. For this belief our forefathers came from Germany to this country of freedom." Helmut shook his head. "How is it they can now say it is against the law to live what we believe?" Looking at Carl, he asked, "Do you understand this?"

"No more than you," he answered, thinking of the books that had been burned and the man named Prager who had been lynched.

"We have word from other Mennonite communities that our boys who have gone to the training camps and refuse to take up arms have suffered terribly."

"They are mistreated?"

Helmut nodded. "They were first told they could request noncombatant service. They were told they would not drill or wear a uniform and that there would be services they could do not in violation of their conscience."

"That's a good plan," Carl said.

"Only a good plan if a plan is followed."

"They lied?"

Helmut nodded, his gentle eyes sad. "Much pressure iss put upon them to be as other soldiers. To prison some have gone."

Carl stared at this boy in disbelief.

Leota touched her brother's arm. "Iss late."

"Ah, so it is. *Verzeih mir.* I mean, forgive me. See? I, too, slip at times." Helmut stood up and gave Leota a hand. "I didn't mean to trouble you," he said.

"That's all right," Carl said. "I was pleased to listen. When I write to my family in Minneapolis, I'll ask them to pray for you."

Leota's blue eyes brightened. "Oh, would you? *Danke schön.*"

"You're welcome." Carl tipped his cap. "I must be going as well. The plow at the blacksmith's is surely ready by now."

Later as the team plodded slowly back to the Mowrys', Carl had plenty of time to think about the Kordzik family and their Mennonite community. The problems he and his family faced seemed small compared to what Helmut and Leota spoke about. He was pleased that he'd decided to stop and talk to them rather than walking away.

When he returned to the farm, Elmer was at the barn and helped him unharness the horses and cool them down.

"You're good with them," Elmer said referring to Streak and Lightning. "They like you."

This was a big compliment coming from Elmer. Mr. Mowry would certainly never say such a thing. When the horses were fed and watered, Elmer helped Carl take the supplies and mail into the house. Once inside the kitchen, Carl pulled out the little sack with the candy.

"Here's something for you and your brother," Carl said,

handing two sticks to Elmer. Turning to Dora, he said, "And one for you as well."

Mrs. Mowry's eyes grew big. She shook her head. "There wasn't enough money for. . ."

"I didn't use your money," Carl said. "I used mine. A gift from me."

Upon hearing that, she seemed to calm down a little. "Eat it up quickly," she said to the children. "Your papa doesn't abide much with frivolous things."

Frivolous things? A stick of candy? What a strange man was Horace Mowry. If this was frivolous, then Carl was even more pleased that he'd indulged the three children.

"Thanks, Carl," Elmer said, his voice all excited. "I'll go find Chester and give him his piece."

"Thank you, Carl," Dora said, looking up at him with wide eyes filled with affection.

One evening about suppertime, a Model T chugged into the Mowry driveway and stopped in front of the house. The man was from the Food Production and Conservation Committee. Mr. Mowry motioned the man in the direction of two cane-bottom chairs situated under the elm tree. Carl heard the man asking Mr. Mowry about the haycutting and the wheat harvest. He wanted to know when it would be ready and how many hands Mr. Mowry thought he would need to get the job done.

As they talked, the man made notes on a clipboard. "The young people will be coming out from the Twin Cities in a week or so," he said. "How many can you board here?"

Mr. Mowry pulled off his soiled hat and scratched his head. "I can fix up a place for five or six out in the barn," he said.

Carl felt the air go out of him. He'd almost forgotten he hadn't come out here for his own comfort or privacy. There was much more work to be done, and it would take more hands than just his to do it.

The two men discussed how the work could be handled in the most efficient manner, and then the man got back in his Model T and drove away in a thick cloud of dust.

Mr. Mowry spat on the ground as he watched the man leave. "Confounded machinery," he said.

The very next day, the boys and Carl joined Mr. Mowry to fix up an area in the barn where several boys could bed down on the floor. They cleaned and swept, and Mr. Mowry even put up a temporary wall. "Just to keep out the rats, cats, and chickens," he muttered around a mouthful of nails.

Carl wondered if he would have to give up his own room, but the subject never came up. Hopefully that meant he wouldn't.

When the Fourth of July arrived, the boys begged their father to be able to go into town for the day. Carl had read the flyer in the window of the general store telling about the festivities. A parade, a carnival, foot races, horse races, and of course fireworks in the evening. All the things that would excite and thrill the children.

But Mr. Mowry wouldn't hear of it. "There's work to be done," he growled. "We have no time for foolishness around here."

Both boys were crestfallen.

The week after the Fourth, they received word that the workers would be arriving on the train the next day. Mr. Mowry and Carl rode into town to fetch them. Dozens of farm wagons and trucks were clustered about the train station because other farmers from the area had also gathered to pick up their workers.

Carl chose to stay in the wagon and wait. He watched as the train pulled to a stop and scores of young boys piled off the train, looking as lost and as green as he'd felt that day when he arrived. But at least these fellows had company. Carl had been all by himself.

There were a few girls in the group. They would be staying at the farmhouses to help with cooking for all these extra farmhands.

The man who had come to the Mowrys' in his Model T stood on a wooden crate on the station platform and addressed the group.

"I'll call out names and assign each young person to a specific farm," he said. "Listen closely as I go down the list."

As Carl listened, he happened to glance again at the door of the train. Gingerly stepping down to the platform was Jillian Oliver, looking prettier than he'd ever remembered her. Her dark hair was fastened in the back with a large hair bow, and a perky little hat sat at an angle on her head. Carl felt his chest go all tight inside.

As he sat wondering if he should try to get her attention, her brother Sidney appeared. Then came Weldon Pritchard. Of all the rotten luck! Carl pulled his cap down and turned away from the platform, hoping he wouldn't be seen.

When the names were called, Sidney and Jillian were assigned to the neighboring farm—the Cramers'. And Weldon Pritchard, along with five other boys, was assigned to Mr. Horace Mowry!

How thankful Carl was that he hadn't tried to pass himself off as Carl *Smith*. He would have never heard the last of it.

CHAPTER 13
Putting Up Hay

Mr. Mowry pointed his six workers in the direction of his wagon. Weldon looked over, then looked again. A smile spread across his face that was more like a sneer. As he approached the wagon, he said to the others, "Well, would you look here. We got us a Kraut."

"Aw, go on," another boy said. "A Kraut for real?"

"Right there sitting on that wagon. Name's Schmidt."

"Schmidt?" came another voice. "Yeah, I recognize him now from school."

Carl's jaw tightened, but he held his peace.

As the boys converged on the wagon, Lightning and Streak grew skittish. Carl took the reins and spoke to them in a low voice to calm them. Their ears flicked back to catch the familiar voice. Carl kept the reins in hand so he'd have something to clench in his fists.

"Say, Sidney," Weldon hollered out to his buddy who was still over by the train. Pointing at Carl, he said, "Look who's here."

Sidney Oliver slapped his forehead in an exaggerated response to the news. This caused Jillian to look over. Her large brown eyes widened in pleasant surprise. She smiled and gave a little wave. Carl nodded. Sidney quickly grabbed her and headed her off toward the Cramers' truck.

"What're you city slickers waiting for? Christmas?" Mr. Mowry's gruff voice sounded from behind the group, sending them scurrying up into the back of the wagon. As he took the reins from Carl's hand, he mumbled, "This has got to be the dumbest idea the government's ever come up with."

As the six boys chattered and talked on the way to the farm, Carl wondered if he might have a slight advantage in this situation. While Mr. Mowry distrusted Carl because he was German, the truth of the matter was, Mr. Mowry distrusted most everyone. Carl at least knew his way around the farm.

The boys had been instructed to bring their bedrolls, and first on the agenda was to get them squared away in their part of the barn. Carl stayed away from the newcomers. He unharnessed the horses, gave them both a good brushing, and turned them loose in the paddock.

Mrs. Mowry set up her "kitchen" on the wide back porch,

where the boys could come by and fill their plates and then eat sitting on the grass in back of the house. Of all the people who needed help, Mrs. Mowry needed it most. Carl wondered why they hadn't requested a girl to come and stay with her. But even as the question formed, he knew the answer. Mr. Mowry no doubt vetoed the idea, saying it wasn't needed.

While the boys were eating, Mr. Mowry told them what was expected of them in the next few weeks. "It's hard work," he told them. "Man's work. If you ain't man enough to do it, let me know right off. We'll take you back to the train station soon's we can get the horses hitched up."

A couple of boys who seemed to be nervous under the burning gaze of Mr. Mowry's steely eyes happened to snicker. The hardened old farmer stopped. "Somethin' funny?"

"Er, no, sir," one stammered.

"Nothing at all," the other added quickly.

Carl had already noticed that those two boys, Clay and Joey, hung close to Wendell Pritchard.

"There's a train coming through tonight and another early in the morning." Mr. Mowry pulled off his shapeless hat, scratched at his scraggly hair, then replaced the hat. "Any one of you could be on it."

When all was quiet again, he resumed explaining about the work to be done. "We get up at five. We'll be in the fields by six. You oversleep, you're on the next train out. Understand?"

There were six nods. Some of them were probably thinking a train ride back to Minneapolis would be welcome about now. Mr. Mowry went on to tell them what was off limits, such as the hog pens and the brooder house. Then he explained the rules about no smoking because of how tinder-dry everything was, and that no one would be let off work for any reason except for broken bones or death-threatening illness.

Carl pitched in and helped Mrs. Mowry with the cleanup work from the meal, then set about to hoe the garden as usual. After Carl had been working about a half hour, Elmer approached him.

"Did you know those fellows are laughing at you? The one with the long nose called you a dumb Kraut and a man-eating Hun."

"Doesn't surprise me."

"I know Papa done that," Elmer continued, "but Papa always calls everybody a name. I don't see no call for them boys to talk like that."

"It's a free country." Carl didn't look up from his hoeing. The corn was beginning to tassel. Mrs. Mowry said they'd have roasting ears in time for the threshing crew. Tomatoes were ripe, and sometimes Carl picked a small one, warm from the summer sun, and bit into it, letting the tangy juice run down his chin.

"I know which bedroll is his," Elmer said, digging his big toe into the soft dirt.

"So?"

"Chester and me could round up a few frogs. . ."

Carl stopped hoeing and looked at Elmer. Suddenly he realized he had a couple of allies. How nice it felt. He smiled at the boy. "Sounds like fun. And I'd even peek through the slats of the barn wall to watch," he said. "But it's not worth it. First of all, they've come out here to do a job for you and your family—they're your guests. Secondly, I'd get blamed, and I don't need any trouble just now."

Elmer nodded. "You're probably right." He turned to go.

"But if you need me and Chester," he added, "just give the nod."

Carl smiled and returned to his work.

The first night the city boys were restless. While Carl's room wasn't right next to the area where the boys bedded down, still the ruckus came through with amazing clarity. They were arm wrestling, playing mumblety-peg with their pocketknives, and generally roughhousing. Presently Carl heard footsteps and snickers outside his window. He rose from his bed and noiselessly stepped to the half-open window and pressed himself against the wall.

His eyes were accustomed to the dark, and he could see their shadows. Just then, a tiny spark flew through the opening of the window. It was a small firecracker. Carl grabbed it as it landed on the floor and instantly threw it back out the window. When it exploded, there were several loud yelps of surprise. Then all was quiet. The footsteps receded.

When he was sure they'd gone back to their own place, Carl grabbed his book, his blanket, and his flashlight and crawled up into the haymow just in case.

The next morning, six very weary boys came dragging up to the back porch to get their breakfast. Two of them had red burn marks on their faces. Mr. Mowry either didn't notice or pretended not to notice.

Carl was ready to do whatever Mr. Mowry told him to do, whether staying with the garden, helping in the kitchen, or working in the hay fields. Mr. Mowry put him in charge of bringing the switchel out to the fields at regular times each day. Switchel, Carl learned, was a mixture of lemonade, molasses, and tea mixed with a little vinegar. It quenched thirst faster and better than water. At least that's what Elmer and Chester told him.

"Too much water'll make a real thirsty man mighty sick," Elmer said. Chester nodded in agreement.

Mr. Mowry cut the hay on the horse-drawn mower, and the boys used pitchforks to make the windrows. The first time Carl rode out with the buckets of switchel, he saw six very red-faced, sweating boys. When Carl rode up with the spring wagon and pulled the horses to a stop, the boys dropped their pitchforks and came swarming around the wagon.

"Finally," said the boy named Joey. "I'm dying of thirst." Pushing ahead of the others, he grabbed a dipper and took a big swig.

Elmer and Chester were elbowing one another as they waited for the first reaction. They weren't disappointed. The mixture came spewing right back out.

"What is this stuff?" he demanded. "It's bitter as gall."

Mr. Mowry strode up. "It's called switchel. Keeps a man from prostrating from heat. Mebbe it don't taste none too good, but it works." He took the dipper from the boy's hand and got himself a drink. "Couple days out here, and you'll come to appreciate it."

Elmer had another dipper in his hand. He handed it to Weldon. Cautiously Weldon took a swallow. He, too, spit it out. "What are you trying to do? Poison us?"

Mr. Mowry drank the remainder of his dipper, handed it back to Chester, and then pointed toward a stand of trees in the distance. "Over yonder's a little crick. You can drink there, if you'd prefer."

"That's where I'm headed," Weldon said. "Anybody here smart enough to go with me?"

As he stomped off, Clay and Joey followed. The others stayed. "I've studied heatstroke," a boy named Matthew said quietly. "I know what you're saying is true." The other three boys drank from the dippers and went back to work.

"Haw there," Carl called to the team. He made a big circle with the wagon to return to the barn.

"Better wait a bit," Elmer said. "We'll need to lay them out under the shade of the wagon for a spell till they get all right again."

Carl wrapped the reins around the brake handle, rested his foot up on the side of the wagon, and waited. It didn't take long. The three boys who had turned down the switchel were writhing and holding their stomachs, sicker than dogs. Chester ran over to them and told them to get under the wagon until they felt better. Carl tried his best not to smile.

There was no uproar in the barn that night, nor the next. The boys were relatively quiet even in the daylight hours. The work was hard and grueling. The sun was hot and relentless. No one had energy for any tomfoolery.

After the hay dried, it was lifted onto wagons. Some of it was then stacked into high mounded haystacks using a canvas sling and a derrick. The rest was put into the haymow using a process that amazed Carl.

First the hay was put on a large flat wooden frame that lay on the ground in front of the barn. As the horses pulled the ropes by a series of pulleys, the frame lifted from the ground all the way up to the opening at the top of the barn. One of the workers stood in the haymow, grabbed the rope, and pulled the frame into the large opening. Then the hay was dumped off, and the empty frame was lowered for another load. This went on all day long until the haymow was nearly full. Carl thought of his engineering-minded brother, Tim. He'd have to tell him about this feat of simple engineering in his next letter.

With so many mouths to feed, more supplies were needed. This meant more trips into town for Carl. Since the government was subsidizing the program of harvest workers, the farm families were allowed a certain amount of food to feed the workers.

One afternoon when Carl was in town, he happened to overhear two men talking just outside the general store. Carl was carrying a bag of flour out to the wagon when he heard the word *Mennonite*. As he heaved the sack into the wagon, he lingered to hear the rest of the conversation. It had something to do with a fire, a fire at the Mennonite meeting house.

Carl shivered in the midday heat. His mind went back to the Prager lynching in Illinois. If it happened in Illinois, it could happen in Minnesota. Before leaving to return to the Mowry farm, he purchased a copy of the local paper to learn more about the fire. There was an article, but it held few details, except to say the meeting house had burned to the ground. The cause of the fire was not determined.

All the way home, Carl worried about Helmut and Leota, wondering if they were safe. If only there were some way he could go and find out for sure.

CHAPTER 14

The Mennonite Colony

Since the workers were given time off on Sunday, Carl had already planned to walk to the Mennonite colony that day. The only trouble was that he didn't know where it was located and to ask would raise plenty of suspicion. More suspicion was something he didn't need.

While the other boys were sleeping in on Sunday morning, Carl still had to get up and milk the cows and slop the hogs. As he worked, he mulled over his problem. There was only one thing to do. He'd have to take Elmer into his confidence. Of course the boy might tell, but it was a chance Carl had to take.

Carl was milking when Elmer came in to help. Elmer grabbed a stool and started milking the cow in the next stanchion. Carl paused and then blurted out his question. "That Mennonite colony where the meeting house burned down. How would a person go about finding that place?"

"You know the crossroads halfway to town where the schoolhouse stands?"

"I remember."

"Turn north there. It's about five miles." They were quiet as the milk zinged into the buckets. The kittens mewed in the corner waiting for their share. "You gonna walk?" Elmer asked.

"Yep."

When they finished, Elmer reached out to take the other bucket. "I'll take 'em to Mama. You best get going."

Carl nodded.

"Carl?"

"Yes."

"I been around them Mennonite people all my life. They never done nothing to hurt nobody."

"I know."

"Can't understand why ever'body's so steamed up at 'em."

"Me neither."

Before Carl could get away, Elmer brought him a canvas-covered canteen full of switchel. "You'll need this," he said.

Carl decided he'd done right by trusting Elmer.

Carl didn't leave by way of the driveway, where he might be seen. Instead he walked along through the pasture for about a half mile, then crawled through the fence and up onto the road. The early morning coolness lasted only a short while. Then the July day turned hot and steamy, with heat shimmering up from the road in waves.

As much as possible, Carl stayed to the side of the road, walking along in the shade of the trees.

As he walked along, he realized he had no idea why he was going to the colony. There was nothing he could do. Something deep inside him just said, "Go."

He hoped he wouldn't meet anyone along the way. If someone asked if he wanted a ride, he certainly couldn't tell them where he was going. When he reached the schoolhouse, he took a minute to sit down under a tree and rest. After drinking a little of the switchel and catching his breath, he continued on his way.

The last mile or so was the worst. By then, the sun was straight overhead. Coming over the brow of a hill, he at last saw the colony spread out before him. A cluster of farms lay across the wide valley with straight strong barns all painted red and neat white houses beside them. The wheat fields were golden, all ready for the harvest. Carl doubted they would have workers from the city to help in their harvest.

In the midst of the beauty was a black scar—the remains of a burned-out building sitting close by the road. As Carl made his way down the hill toward the colony, he saw a crowd of people gathered under a grove of walnut trees near the rubble. It looked as though a picnic were in progress.

Sure enough, tables were spread with good food. Carl could smell the delicious aromas before he was within a hundred yards. As he left the road to head in their direction, he heard a voice call out his name. It was Helmut!

"Carl Schmidt! You come to us," he said as he strode toward Carl's side. He clapped Carl's shoulder and shook his hand.

"I heard about the fire."

Helmut's face sobered. "Yes, the fire. Terrible it was. Our lovely meeting house all destroyed. But we can build again. Come now," he said, his face lit up once again. "You will meet Papa and Mama and the other families."

Leota, surrounded by several other smiling red-cheeked girls, came running up to greet him. Helmut guided him toward the cluster of people, all of whom were dressed in traditional plain clothes—the men with their flat-brimmed hats and the ladies with their small white lace caps. They seemed overjoyed to see Carl, as though greeting a long lost friend. A gray-bearded man by the name of Jervis Luscher seemed to be a leader and spokesman in the group. He grasped Carl's hand and thanked him for caring enough to come. They seemed amazed that he'd walked all that way.

Helmut's father, Bertram Kordzik, reminded Carl of his own papa with his quiet manner and kind smile. He introduced his shy wife, Agathe, who quickly brought lemonade to the boy.

Carl caused a general hubbub in the quiet Sunday afternoon picnic. The Mennonites made sure his plate was full and that he ate every bite, and yet they asked questions while he was trying to eat. He told them of his father and how Papa had disassociated himself early on from the German Americans who were in favor of the Kaiser's actions. Then he explained how Papa had been under suspicion of sabotage at the flour mill and spent a night in jail. Carl wasn't aware he could talk so much at one time, but these people seemed to pull things out of him.

Then they shared stories of their sons and brothers who were being persecuted in the army camps.

"Like our Savior Jesus," one elderly lady said, her aged

face lined with creases and wrinkles. "For loving peace they suffer and for doing harm to no man."

Bertram Kordzik nodded as he stroked his beard. "We are told in the Scriptures that we would partake of Christ's sufferings."

"Tell me about the fire," Carl said as he pushed back an empty plate. "Did you see who did it?"

Jervis Luscher scowled. "Like veasels after der *Hühnchens*! In and out they slip in der darkness."

"Like weasels after our chickens," Helmut interpreted. Carl nodded.

"Neighbors ve have loved," Mr. Luscher continued, "with them ve have lived for decades, now see us as enemies." He shook his head. "It may be to Canada ve must go for a time."

Carl set down his empty glass, which was quickly filled again with more lemonade. "Canada?"

"Vat else could ve do?"

"What would happen to the farms?" Carl asked. "Your belongings?"

"Those are just things," Bertram Kordzik put in. "Lives are more important than things. With God's help, we can begin again when we return."

When the picnic things were cleared away, the people clustered together. Jervis Luscher prayed for them and for their safety, and then he prayed for Carl and the Schmidt family.

Helmut insisted that Carl come to their house for a short time before starting back. Carl glanced up at the sun, which was quickly moving over into midafternoon. When he hesitated, Helmut said to his father, "Could I not take Carl a ways in the buggy? No one would see."

Mr. Kordzik patted his son on the shoulder. "A wise plan, Helmut. Taking the trail through the fields will cut the distance in half."

So it was decided. Carl walked with them to their simple well-scrubbed home. The walks were lined by rainbows of flowers, and under each window flower boxes spilled over with brilliant red geraniums. Every blossom spoke of love and care. The Mowry farm seemed slovenly in comparison.

"War breeds hate," Mr. Kordzik said, sounding even more like Carl's papa. They were sitting comfortably in the Kordzik's tidy parlor. "One must hate in order to kill another. Or even to wish another to be dead. Ach," he said shaking his head, "though the guns be across the ocean, the hate multiplies on our own doorstep."

The visit wasn't all about war. Funny stories were shared, and laughter sounded in the Kordzik household, just as it did in the Schmidt home. When it was time for him to leave, Carl went to the barn with Helmut and Mr. Kordzik and helped to hitch their fine high-stepping horse to the black enclosed buggy.

After Carl had said good-bye to the rest of the family, Helmut guided the buggy away from the road and through a pasture. If Carl had known there were such clear wide trails through the fields, it would have saved him several miles of walking.

When Helmut stopped the buggy, Carl could see the schoolhouse in the distance. "To take you farther would endanger you and me," he said, "though I wish to the door of the Mowry home I could take you."

"Thank you, Helmut. God bless you."

"And you my friend." Helmut reached out his hand and gripped Carl's firmly.

Carl stepped down then, almost swallowed up in tall ripe wheat on both sides. He walked away without looking back.

When Carl reached the Mowry farm, it was nearly suppertime. The timing was perfect. He'd returned in time to do the evening chores. As he approached the barn, Weldon stepped out from behind a rock wall and stood directly in front of him.

"Where've you been?" he demanded.

Carl attempted to step around him, but the bigger boy stopped him by putting out a long arm and shoving against his chest. "Oh no, you don't. I asked a question. Where've you been all day?"

"Church." That wasn't a total lie. The Mennonites had just finished church when he arrived, and they did pray.

Weldon narrowed his eyes. "Liar. You went to see those other Krauts. The ones who wear the funny clothes with no buttons. I heard you talking to the Mowry kid early this morning."

Carl grew concerned. Perhaps he shouldn't have involved Elmer after all. Was the boy in trouble?

"Birds of a feather flock together, as the old saying goes," Weldon went on in a taunting tone. "All you clannish Krauts gotta pal around with each other. Well, this is just dandy. I've been wondering how to get rid of you, and you played right into my hands."

He stepped around Carl like a barn cat tormenting a mouse. "You're always acting so hoity-toity just because you can hitch up those old nags and can milk a few cows. Well, as soon as old man Mowry hears what you did, he'll have you on the next train out of here."

Carl looked at Weldon. "And you'll be right beside me on the same train."

"Me? Why me? I haven't done anything. I stayed right here all day."

"Smoking's forbidden anywhere around the barns."

"What're you talking about? I've never smoked around here."

"No?" Carl's voice was cool. "You've seen my camera. I took photographs of you from up there in the haymow. Real clear shots. I'm a pretty good photographer."

"You're lying. Let me see the picture."

"Right this way." Carl led him around the barn to his room, slipped inside, and dragged his photo box out from under his bed. After digging out the photo he was looking for, he went back out and showed it to Weldon. The shot included not only Weldon, but Joey and Clay, all puffing on cigarettes just a few feet from the back of the barn.

Just as Carl suspected, Weldon's long arm reached out and grabbed it. "You *did* have a picture of me," he said, laughing as he tore it up into little pieces. "It's gone now."

Carl turned to go back into his room. "For your information, Pritchard, I never make only one copy of any print. There are several more where that one came from."

When he reached his door to go inside, Carl turned and saw that Weldon Pritchard was gone. As he changed into his work clothes, he could hardly believe his own quick thinking. Or that he'd actually stood up to that bully.

CHAPTER 15
Threshing Time

Wheat harvest was much different than the haying. The big steam-driven threshers moved from farm to farm, and the workers traveled with them so that every wheat field could be harvested. First the wheat was cut and bundled into shocks and left to dry. Using pitchforks, the workers slung the sheaves into the threshing machine, which separated the grain from the straw.

It took many hands to do the work and much food to feed them all. There must have been eight or nine women all crowded in the kitchen the day they converged at the Mowry farm. Carl had nearly forgotten that this meant he'd be seeing Jillian again.

As before, Carl and the younger boys were the ones who took the switchel out to the workers. Only now they also transported the galvanized water tank that held the water necessary to keep the steam engine running. It took many trips from the pump at the concrete watering tank next to the barn out to where the noisy, chugging steam-driven threshers were located.

After their second trip that morning, Carl went to the house for another bucket of switchel. Jillian stood alone out in the yard, spreading tablecloths across the plank tables.

A sudden attack of shyness gripped Carl as he started to walk past her. He wasn't sure he should be seen talking to her. But even more, he had no idea what to say to her. His heart was pounding, and his tongue felt as though it were glued to the roof of his mouth.

"Good morning, Carl. Aren't you going to say hello?" Her voice sounded like a little melody.

He stopped. "Hello, Jillian."

"Would you take that corner of the tablecloth? It's too far for me to reach across."

He set down the empty buckets and did as she asked, even though he knew she could have spread the cloth herself.

"Do you like living on a farm?" she asked, her soft, warm eyes smiling at him.

He nodded as he straightened his side of the tablecloth.

She reached down and unfolded another cloth and flung it out over the end of the plank table. "Cat got your tongue? You never talk much, do you?"

"I do when I have to." He thought of how he'd talked Weldon down a few days before.

"I saw you working with the horses. You have a way with them, don't you?"

Carl was astonished that she'd noticed. Something made him wish he could tell her how he felt deep down inside about the horses. How he'd learned to be quiet around them and sense what they were feeling and what they needed. How he talked to them in the night, and how they came to him whenever he called to them. But how could he say all that? And would she even understand?

He started to say that he liked horses very much, when Elmer came up behind them. "I wondered what was taking you so long. We better get a move on or Papa'll be real mad."

"Excuse me," Carl said to Jillian, smoothing the last of the wrinkles from his side of the tablecloth. "See you at lunchtime." Grabbing the buckets, he hurried inside to get them filled.

As they were driving back out to the field, Elmer said, "That girl is real pretty. Does she go to your school?"

"She does."

"You like her?"

Carl thought about that a minute. "Yeah, Elmer, I do."

At lunch, Sidney kept close watch on his sister. There was no opportunity for Carl to speak to Jillian again the rest of that day. The thresher was at the Mowry farm for two days, and then it moved to the next farm, the Cramer place.

Once he was away from the Mowry farm, Carl was just another member of the threshing crew. He wielded his pitch-fork in the hot sun and drank the switchel along with the rest. But he rather enjoyed putting his body through the rigorous work. He could almost feel his muscles strengthening and his stamina increasing.

When they broke for the noon meal, tables loaded with food waited for them in the yard. Jillian went around filling glasses with water or lemonade and filling tin cups with more coffee. When she came to where Carl was sitting with his back propped up against a shade tree, she stopped to talk, asking him about the harvest.

Instantly Sidney stepped over and said, "Schmidt, you've been told not to talk to my sister. I knew you were a dumb Kraut. Maybe you're a deaf one as well."

Slowly Carl set his plate aside and stood up. "I believe your sister was speaking to me," he said evenly. "Her choice. It's a free country, you know."

Sidney turned to Jillian. "Stay away from this Hun or I'll see to it you're sent home."

Jillian lowered her eyes and moved on to fill another glass with her pitcher of lemonade, clearly embarrassed by his outburst.

Just then, Elmer sidled up to Carl. "Papa wants you out in the barn," he said.

Carl picked up his plate and glass and took them over to Jillian. "Thank you, Jillian," he said loudly enough for Sidney to hear. "Would you take these, please?"

"I'd be happy to," she answered, smiling.

Carl strode off behind Elmer. "What does Mr. Mowry want?" he asked when they were out of earshot of the others.

"Nothin'," the boy said over his shoulder. "But I didn't want to see that barrel-chested fella put you on your backside in front of all those people."

Carl laughed. What a kid! Maybe someday, if he ever got away from his domineering father, Elmer Mowry would become a congressman or an attorney.

The threshing lasted about two weeks, spending two days at each farm. All the young folk were talking about the get-together that the Food Production and Conservation Committee planned for them after the harvest was in. A party and dance were to be held on the main street of Spencerville. Carl had already made up his mind he wouldn't join them. It was bad enough being around Weldon and Sidney while working. A social event with them would be unbearable.

The farmers, who talked incessantly about the weather, were grateful there'd been no rain to slow down the work. Actually there'd not been any rain to speak of for several weeks, and dust coated everything. Carl felt like he'd eaten a whole wheelbarrow of dirt just from working out in it all day.

Late one evening, a huge thunderhead piled up on the horizon in the east. However, it melted away almost as fast as it rose up. But not before Carl was able to snap several photographs of it from the haymow. He wanted to capture the fascinating slivers of heat lightning as it streaked through the dark clouds.

On the last day of threshing, the workers were eating their noon meal at the last farm, when an automobile drove up. Not an old Model T, but a nice automobile. Out stepped a man in an army uniform. In his hand was an envelope. The entire crowd fell silent.

The officer took in the gathering. Carl didn't envy him his job.

"Is there a Gerald Shipley here?"

Carl heard Mrs. Shipley gasp, and several of the women rushed to her side.

Gerald Shipley stepped forward. "I'm Shipley."

"I'm sorry to inform you, sir. Your son, Corporal Randall Shipley, was killed in action in Chateau-Thierry, France, on July 10, 1918." He handed Mr. Shipley the ominous-looking envelope.

Mrs. Shipley was sobbing and wailing. "No, no. Please no. Not my Randy! Not my darling Randy."

The women helped her into the house. Mr. Shipley stared dumbly at the envelope in his hand.

Carl was never sure how they finished out the rest of the day. As he heaved pitchforks full of grain up into the thresher, he thought about Truman. Then he thought about Greg Hastings and all the other boys who were over there fighting. How many would have to die before it was all over?

Mrs. Mowry chose to stay on at the Shipleys' for the night to lend support. She kept Dora with her. Several of the other wives also stayed since Mrs. Shipley was beside herself with grief.

Carl was surprised later that afternoon when Mr. Mowry said he was taking the wagon back into town to the shindig, as he called it. From what Carl knew of Mr. Mowry, he assumed there'd be no shindig for his workers.

The boys washed in the stock tank, changed into clean clothes, and slicked their hair back with good-smelling Hair Slik, then crawled into the back of the wagon. Even Elmer and Chester were all cleaned up and sitting on the wagon seat beside their papa. No one seemed to notice that Carl wasn't among them.

After they left, Carl took his book and camera up to the haymow. Now that it was filled with hay, it was more difficult to get around. But he made a little nest for himself. The aroma from the fresh cut hay was one he'd remember for the rest of his life. It smelled sweet and clean and good.

Another thunderhead was piling up on the horizon. This one looked to be packing more punch than the one a few nights ago.

Carl tried to read, but his mind was on the horrible news of the death of the Shipley boy. A fine young farm boy. His mama and papa would never even see his grave. Perhaps they'd never know where it was located. Carl couldn't imagine anything sadder than that.

Cradled in the soft hay, he never knew when he fell asleep, but a loud crack of thunder woke him. Then he heard a wagon come rattling up the drive. Hurriedly he crawled through the mounds of hay to look out the opening that faced the house. It wasn't until the lightning flashed again that he could see it was the Mowrys' wagon. But Elmer was driving. Beside him sat Jillian Oliver. What was Jillian doing riding with Elmer Mowry?

Carl jumped across the hay and scrambled down the ladder as fast as he could go.

CHAPTER 16
Mob Violence

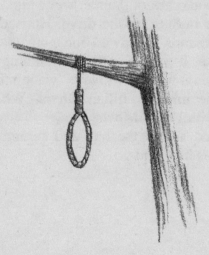

"Elmer!" Carl called out. The wind whipped up and blew dirt in his eyes. "What's the matter?"

"Papa's drunker'n a hoot owl," Elmer said. "All the men are. It's an awful sight."

So that's why Mr. Mowry was so willing to go to town.

"We heard them talking," Jillian said. "They're going to the Mennonite community. They're talking about doing awful things."

"Are you sure? Maybe it's all talk."

"I've seen a mob before," Elmer told him. "And this is a mob!"

"It's all being riled up by Mr. Shipley," Jillian added. "He's asking why his boy should fight and die and those Mennonites get to keep their boys home. It's a terrible, frightening anger."

"Can you take me to the colony?" Carl asked Elmer.

"Sorry. I have to get back fast. We took a big chance just getting away to come here."

"But somebody has to warn them," Carl said. "I'll never make it there on time."

Another gust of wind whipped Jillian's dark hair wildly about her head. She pushed it out of her face.

"Ride Dale." Elmer held the reins tightly as another crack of thunder frightened the team. "Dale's the gentler one. Put the halter on him and go. He'll do anything for you. I've seen him."

"But your Papa'd be furious."

"He may never know. Anyway, seems to me it'd be worth the risk."

Without another word, Elmer turned the wagon around.

Jillian waved and called out, "I'll be praying for you, Carl." Then they were gone.

Carl raced to the corral, grabbed the halter, and put it over Dale's head. Then he led the horse out. "I need your help, boy. There's a whole slew of people needing your help."

He crawled up on the fence to get astride the broad back. "I'm counting on you, fella. Don't fail me." Once they were on the road, he put the horse into an easy lope. He knew the giant could go for hours at that speed and never tire.

Carl now knew to take the trails through the fields. By

the time he crested the hill overlooking the Mennonite community, fat splashes of raindrops were hitting his face. "Come on, boy," he said digging his heels in. "This isn't exactly like a William S. Hart flicker, but it's close."

Down the hill they went with Carl shouting at the top of his voice.

People ran out of their houses to see what the commotion was all about. Bertram Kordzik and Jervis Luscher reached him first. "A mob's coming!" Carl yelled. "You've got to get out. Right away."

The rain was pelting down. Mr. Kordzik ran to the big bell in the center of the intersection by the burned-out church. Pulling the rope, he sent it clanging over and over until every person in the valley was alerted.

"A good plan ve have," Mr. Luscher told him. "To use it this soon, we did not know. The vimmen and der children take buggies north to New Ulm. There the station master's our friend. They board der train to Canada. The men and boys load our belongings into wagons. Keeping to the back roads our escape will be made. It vill vork, you think?"

Carl had no idea if it would work or not. "They're all drunk," Carl told him.

"Drunk can mean blind rage," the older man said, "but ve pray it means *blind*, period."

"May I help you?" Carl asked.

"Ah, my son, you have helped," Mr. Luscher said. "More than you vill ever ever know. The owner of this horse, he does not know you're borrowing him. It is so? Best you get back."

Carl reached down to shake the man's hand. As he did, Helmut came running out to him with a rain slicker. "Put this on, Carl. With our blessings."

Carl grabbed the slicker and put it over him, pulling the

hood up to protect his head. Even in their danger, the Mennonites thought of others. "Thank you, Helmut. God bless you."

By the time Carl reached the main road on the far side of the schoolhouse, rain was pouring down in torrents. But in the slippery mud, Dale's wide feet were as sure as a mountain goat's.

Inside the warm barn, Carl washed the big horse down and dried him thoroughly. Then he brought Clyde in out of the pouring rain as well. He dried him down and put them both in separate stalls for the night.

The rain poured down all through the night. Carl lay on his small cot, but sleep wouldn't come. He prayed for the Mennonite families. Could they make it through this awful deluge? Then his thoughts turned to Jillian. Why had she come with Elmer? He'd felt all along that she had a tender heart. Now he was sure his feelings had been correct. What a very special girl she was.

Mr. Mowry and the wagonload of drenched boys didn't come into the driveway until nearly dawn. The rain had slacked off to a steady drizzle. Carl could hear them singing and laughing. Obviously the boys had done some drinking right along with the menfolk.

Carl was up at his regular time, getting the chores done. Elmer came into the barn just as he was taking the milk stool down from the peg.

"It was quite a sight," he said softly. "Wish you coulda seen it. Trucks and wagons all in a long line on the road out from town. But all them little cricks was flooded, and they kept getting stuck. They unhitched horses from wagons to pull the trucks out of the mud. What a sight."

Elmer chuckled as he took down the other milking stool. "Then when we finally got to the Mennonites' farms, wasn't nobody there. Not a soul. Those drunk fellows was so mad they tried to set fires, but the fires kept going out because of the rain."

He sat on the stool and began to milk. "I can't rightly remember seeing nothing so funny as those drunken men trying to strike matches in the rain and swearing 'cause they was going out fast as they could light 'em."

Carl smiled at the thought. Silently he wondered if God sent that rainstorm in order to protect those innocent Mennonites.

"Jillian?" Carl asked. "Is she all right?"

"I left her off at the Cramers' on my way back to town."

"Thanks, Elmer."

"Don't mention it."

The city boys had yet another day at the farm before they were scheduled to take the train back home. Carl would be staying on another three weeks. Weldon seemed to suspect Carl had something to do with the Mennonites getting away. He hinted around about it, but Carl ignored him.

On the last day, Mr. Mowry made sure he was getting all the work out of the boys that he possibly could. Each one was given a job around the place.

That afternoon, Carl was picking the sweet corn for Mrs. Mowry when Elmer came up behind him in the row of head-high corn and said, "I think Chester and me got just what you been waiting for."

"What's that?"

"Come and see."

Knowing Elmer, Carl wouldn't have dreamed of saying

no. He put the basket of sweet corn on the back porch and followed Elmer to the corral behind the barn. Weldon stood inside the corral, shoveling manure into the spreader.

Carl looked at Elmer and smiled. Chester was crouched behind the fence at the gate that led to the pasture. Carl jumped up on the wooden fence. "Weldon! Look out," he yelled. "It's the bull! He's coming right for you!"

Chester had opened the gate. Mack came dutifully trotting to where he knew the feed bin was located. Weldon took one look at the bull coming toward him and crumpled in a heap on the ground. "No, no! Help! Don't let him get me." He was crying like a baby.

Climbing over the fence, Carl leaped into the corral. "That's all right, Weldon. I won't let him get you." He ran up to the old bull, put his arm around his neck, and guided him over to the feed bunk. "Good old Mack. You hungry? Is that it? Here you go. Nice feed for good old Mack."

Weldon stared in disbelief. Slowly he got to his feet. "You won't tell anybody about this, will you?"

Carl looked over the bull's back at Weldon. "What was that you said, Weldon?" he asked.

"You won't tell. . .I mean about how I. . ."

Carl shrugged. "I won't if you won't."

At the train station, Carl had only a fleeting glimpse of Jillian as she boarded to go home. She mouthed, "See you at school." He nodded and touched his hand to his cap.

Weldon could no longer look Carl in the eyes, and Carl knew the tables had been turned.

August moved along hot, dry, and uneventful. For as much as Carl loved the country, he grew more homesick the closer the time came for him to leave. Letters from his family let him know they were more than ready for him to return home.

Carl also missed getting daily news of the war. The next time he was in Spencerville, he grabbed a Minneapolis newspaper. It told of amazing victories by the Allies. One article reported that since the American divisions had fought so well in every battle, General Pershing wanted a separate American army to be formed. General Ferdinand Foch, the French general who served as the Allied Commander in Chief, agreed. The American First Army became official on August 10, 1918.

Yet another article reported that on August 8, the British had attacked in the Somme area, along with two divisions of U.S. troops. The British used several hundred tanks to break through a mass of barbed wire that had been created by the Germans for protection. The Germans were taken by complete surprise, and thousands of prisoners were taken.

Carl was driving back from town in the wagon as he read this news. Thousands of Germans taken prisoner? How very different this was from the first years of the conflict. Could this mean the war was nearly over?

The morning Carl was scheduled to leave, he rose and did the chores as usual. It seemed no different than any other morning. He gave the horses extra loving care and talked to them softly, letting each one know how much he'd miss them. He'd shot plenty of photographs, though. That way, he'd always remember them.

He looked around at the farm machinery that filled the farmyard adjacent to the barn. He now knew the difference between the rake, the harrow, the planter, and the mower, and of course he was well acquainted with the manure spreader.

Not much was said at breakfast. Mr. Mowry instructed everyone to be ready to leave for town directly after the table was cleared. As the man stood and grabbed his hat and scrunched it on his head, Carl heard him mumble, "You'd think they'd come up with a way to have this thing last all year long."

The thing he referred to must have meant Carl's stay. The comment was as close to a compliment as Carl had ever heard from the man.

In his room, Carl swept the floor and made up the cot. He took the rain slicker, rolled it up tightly, and shoved it down into the valise with the rest of his belongings. That rain slicker would always hold special meaning for Carl. He glanced around at the small room, then slowly closed the door.

Elmer and Chester helped harness Lightning and Streak. "First we had to say good-bye to Arthur and Foster," Chester said with a tight voice. "Now we have to say good-bye to you. Don't hardly seem fair."

"Good-bye doesn't have to mean forever," Carl told him. Chester didn't answer. Carl knew his words were hollow. Chester was feeling what Carl had felt when Truman went away. And what Larry had felt at Greg's leaving. That awful feeling of separation was being experienced by thousands of families all over the nation whose boys were called away to fight the war.

At the station, Mrs. Mowry and the children waited with Carl on the platform, but Mr. Mowry chose to stay in the wagon. Carl didn't try to figure it out, nor did he let it bother him. Mr. Mowry was who he was. No one could change that.

As the train chugged into the station and ground to a stop, suddenly Dora was clinging to him and crying. Crying loudly. No amount of hushing from her mama could still it.

"I'm gonna miss you, Carl," she said between sobs. "You saved my Fancy, and I'll never never forget you." He reached down to put his arms around her and return her hug, swallowing the lump in his throat.

Then Mrs. Mowry had her arms around his neck, and she kissed his cheek. "You're a good boy, Carl. A good boy." Never had he seen a display of affection from this woman in all the months he'd known her.

Elmer stretched out his hand. "Good-bye Carl." Carl ignored the hand and gave him a big bear hug, making him cry. Then he did the same with Chester.

As the "all aboard" was called out, Carl grabbed up his valise, ran to the train, and hopped on. He waved to the teary-eyed family as the train began to move forward. Then he happened to glance over at the wagon. Mr. Horace Mowry tipped his hat.

CHAPTER 17

Back Home

Not even a decorated war hero deserved the kind of home-coming Carl received at the Minneapolis train station that evening. All his family was there, along with the Allertons and the Moes. There was hugging and laughing and crying and more carrying on than he'd seen in a long time. He was hugged and kissed and his back patted until he was almost sore. But it was wonderful. They went on and on about how tall and strong and tanned he looked.

Uncle Erik had purchased a car since Carl had been away, so they were loaded up in two automobiles and whisked away to the Allertons' for a big picnic. Carl stuffed himself until he could hardly eat another bite. He'd forgotten just how good his mama and his two aunts could cook.

When everything had calmed down somewhat, Papa said, "Tell me, Carl, do you know anyone who lives in Canada?"

The late August air was still and warm. There was a fragrance of newly cut grass in the air. Carl's mind was whirling a million miles a second. "I'm not sure. Why?"

Papa pulled out a letter from his coat pocket. "Someone who wrote this letter lives in Canada. Says they know you."

"How in the world. . .?"

"What kind of secrets are you keeping, Carl?" Uncle Erik asked with a grin on his face.

"The way we hear it," Tim put in, "you're something of a hero. Were you going to tell us?"

Carl shook his head in disbelief. Papa unfolded the letter. "This letter came addressed to 'Hans Schmidt, father of Carl Schmidt,' and is signed by several people."

So they made it. They made it after all. A deep sigh escaped Carl's lips. "May I see the letter?"

But Papa began reading aloud:

Dear Mr. Hans Schmidt,

We are writing to commend your very brave and courageous son, Carl, who warned our entire community of an impending attack by a drunken mob. We were already making preparations to leave since conditions were becoming unbearable. However, that night we would have had no warning except that your son rode a workhorse bareback through a terrible thunderstorm to warn us. His warning and the God-sent thunderstorm ensured our safe escape. While we may have few possessions remaining when

*we return to our farms, not a life was lost, and that
is most important.*

*May we commend you, Mr. Schmidt, on having
brought up a good son who has the love of God in
his heart. You can be very proud of him.*

When Papa finished reading the letter, Carl was surprised
to find that his cheeks were wet. The entire family burst into
cheers, and he got about a hundred more hugs. The whole
thing was simply too amazing to comprehend. All he could
think of was the violence that might have occurred had the
Mennonites not gotten away. How many lynchings might
there have been that night? No one would ever know.

Stilt and Winkie and the other newsboys were excited to
see Carl back again. The two schoolboys who'd taken his
route during the summer weren't as kind, they said, nor as
friendly as Carl. His customers along the route were also
glad to see him return. They waved to him from their front
doors, and some pulled back lace curtains to give a friendly
wave. A businessman on his way to catch the trolley tipped
his hat and said, "Good morning, Carl. Welcome home."

As he rode his bicycle through the early morning still-
ness, flinging newspapers onto the porches with amazing
accuracy, it felt very good to be home. Perhaps one day he
might live in the country, where a person could see all the
sky at once and all the stars in the black night, but for now
it was just good to be home.

On Sunday Carl was back in church with his family.
Never had the hymns sounded so good to his ears, and he
even paid attention to every word of the pastor's sermon.

Unlike when he went away, the newspapers were now
filled with blaring black headlines of victories. The St. Mihiel

campaign began on September 12 and ended with overwhelming success on September 16. The newspaper said more
than half a million American troops had taken part. Carl could
not comprehend that many armed men shooting and being
shot at. When the offensive ended, the Germans had been
driven entirely out of the area they had only recently taken.

This particular battle was of interest to cousin Larry
since more than six hundred aircraft took part, many of
which were bombers.

Larry's photo collection in the playroom had expanded
greatly. When he could get Carl alone, Larry showed off his
most recent additions. Larry explained that a colonel by the
name of Billy Mitchell was made Chief of the Air Service,
First Army.

"But Eddie Rickenbacker is still my greatest hero,"
Larry said. "He's now the ace of all aces! He's shot down
twenty-six enemy aircraft."

Remembering how queasy he'd felt riding the train, Carl
couldn't imagine speeding along through the skies, turning
flips and loops and nosedives as these pilots did day after day.

By the time school opened in September, newspapers were
also filled with reports of a frightening illness on the East
Coast. Hundreds of people were dying from it. Soon the
influenza was spreading across the nation. People were
dying everywhere.

Carl found life at school virtually unchanged. German-
American students were still being shunned. He'd hoped
some of the Allied victories might have changed all that.
But as Papa often said, "Once hate begins, it's nearly impossible to stop."

In Carl's social studies class, the teacher suggested that

the Spanish flu was a plot of the German Americans to get back at the United States for entering the war. When Carl reported this idea to the family at supper, Papa said, "They say whatever makes them feel better no matter how insane it may seem."

Smoothing his mustache with his hand, he continued, "Something like the flu is unknown and frightening. They wonder, 'Could God be doing this?' No, no. Couldn't be God. Then who? Ah, the easiest answer. Someone we hate. Must be the Germans.' "

Each morning at school, rather than waiting for Jillian to speak to him, Carl went out of his way to greet her. One evening he stayed up late writing a letter to her. It would be easier to tell her in a letter how much he appreciated her coming to tell him about the mob. Truth be told, she and Elmer were the real heroes on that stormy night. The next morning he mustered his courage to step right up to her and hand her the letter. She was wearing a yellow dress, and her dark hair looked clean and glossy as it spilled over her shoulders.

"This is for you," he said, putting the letter in her hand.

Several girls who stood nearby giggled and snickered, but it didn't bother Carl one bit.

"Thank you, Carl," Jillian said.

Just as Carl reached the end of the hall, Sidney stepped out and grabbed him forcefully by the collar, nearly knocking him off his feet. "Listen, Kraut," Sidney hissed through clenched teeth. "I've told you to stay away from my sister. You don't seem to hear very well. This is the last time."

One of Sidney's friends standing nearby said, "We know you Krauts started this infernal epidemic. And my papa's sick in bed with it right this minute. If he dies. . ." He didn't finish the sentence.

"Never could trust a Hun," Joey said, coming up behind Carl. "Never could, never will."

"He's right," Sidney agreed. "From now on, Schmidt, you better keep a close watch over your shoulder." With that he gave Carl a rough shove, spun on his heel, and stomped off.

Carl had never been in a fistfight before. He'd avoided them all his life. He figured in a fair fight he might be able to put Sidney down. But he didn't really figure Sidney would fight fair.

His figuring was correct. Just a few blocks from school that afternoon, Sidney and four of his chums jumped out from behind a hedgerow and stood directly in front of Carl. Two of the boys were Joey and Clay.

Carl felt his heart begin to trip double-time. His mouth went bone dry, and his hands grew clammy. "Does it take four of you? Am I that big a threat?"

"You've been asking for this for a long time," Sidney snarled, "and I've been aching to give it to you."

He took a step forward. At the same instant, Carl threw his chemistry book at the boy next to Sidney, hitting him in the cheek, then he ducked as Sidney took a swing. Carl stood up in time to land a hard uppercut to Sidney's jaw with his right. He felt the impact up to his shoulder and heard Sidney let out a groan.

That was probably the last lick he'd get in. Quickly Joey and Clay whipped in behind him and grabbed his arms, twisting them painfully behind his back.

Sidney had caught his breath and was just ready to step forward and take a good hard swing when a voice sounded behind them. "What's going on here?"

It was Weldon Pritchard.

CHAPTER 18

It's Over!

Carl twisted and pulled to get his arms loose while the boys were distracted by Weldon's appearance, but he was held fast.

"You goof," Sidney said sharply. "What do you think's going on?"

Weldon stepped between Sidney and Carl. "I think it's a very unfair fight, that's what I think."

"Get out of the way, Pritchard," Sidney ordered.

"You standing up for a Kraut, Pritchard?" Joey said in a sneer. "This guy's been bothering Sid's sister. And besides, these Huns are the ones who've started the flu. You know that, don't you?"

Weldon continued to stand between them. Carl felt the boys loosen their hold on his arms.

"Seems to me Jillian's old enough and smart enough to know who she wants to talk to," Weldon said. He turned and gave Joey and Clay a hard push. Carl's arms were free. He rubbed at his sore wrists.

"Furthermore," Weldon went on, not raising his voice, "if this terrible Hun here helped spread flu germs, what in the world are you doing getting this close to him? You're probably already infected!"

"I didn't mean he actually *did* it," Sidney said, stumbling over his words.

"Just what did you mean?"

"I mean he's probably somehow connected to those who did it."

Weldon put his arm around Carl's shoulder. "Sidney, why don't you admit you haven't the slightest idea what you're trying to say about my friend here. Now go on and leave him alone."

"You'll be sorry, Weldon Pritchard, siding with the enemy like this." As Sidney spoke, he began walking away. The others followed.

When they were gone, Weldon picked up the chemistry book, dusted it off, and handed it to Carl. "I believe this is yours."

"Thanks, Weldon. Thanks a lot."

"Don't mention it. I don't think he'll bother you anymore."

Stars on the service flags throughout the city turned from blue to gold with amazing rapidity as hundreds of American boys bled and died on the battlefields of France. But the war was definitely turning around.

138

Names of the heroes were becoming almost as well known as movie idols around the nation. One was Lieutenant Colonel Charles Whittlesey, the commander of the "Lost Battalion," who refused to surrender even when he realized his entire battalion was surrounded by Germans.

Then there was Corporal Alvin York, who single-handedly captured 132 Germans, killed about 20, and silenced about 40 machine guns. York was a simple mountaineer from Tennessee, but he was an expert marksman.

Bulgaria and Turkey were now out of the war. Turkey surrendered on October 30, bringing an end to the great Ottoman Empire.

These stories were running in the newspapers side by side with the increasing numbers of deaths from the nightmarish flu. Dozens of teachers had been stricken, which forced the Minneapolis school board to close down school altogether. No one even attempted to estimate when it would reopen. At the moment, that didn't matter. Uncle Richard was on the go day and night as he worked to help the flu victims.

While Carl didn't miss going to school, he certainly missed seeing Jillian. He thought about her most of his waking moments and began praying that the dreaded flu wouldn't touch her home or her.

Carl devoted himself to his photography and to getting the garden ready to be put to bed for the winter. The family had done a good job of taking care of the victory garden while he was away, but they were more than happy to give the work back to him upon his return.

On November 1, Uncle Erik telephoned as the Schmidts were eating supper. Mama talked to him. Word had just come in over the wire that the American troops had broken through the Hindenburg Line. This was the line that had been established at the beginning of the war in 1914.

"It has broken the Germans' main railroad supply line," Uncle Erik practically shouted into the phone. They could all hear him. "There's word that the German forces have revolted and mutinied. It's as good as over."

Carl was so excited he could hardly eat. "Over." The word reverberated in his head. Just like Uncle Richard's favorite song said: *And we won't come back till it's over over there.* . . .

A couple days later Austria-Hungary surrendered. Papa said it was like a house of cards collapsing one on top of the other.

CHAPTER 19

Armistice Day

The telephone woke everyone at three in the morning. Carl sat straight up in bed.

"Go back to sleep," Tim mumbled. "It's just another prank call."

Carl was certain it wasn't. He bounded out of bed and ran downstairs. It was Uncle Erik. Papa was at the telephone, barefooted and in his flannel nightshirt. His face was wreathed in a smile.

Putting his hand over the mouthpiece, he turned to Carl. "The Kaiser has abdicated and fled to Holland. The armistice will be signed at eleven o'clock this morning at Compiègne in France."

Carl let out a whoop that brought the whole family running. When the news was announced, even Mama was jumping up and down and shouting along with the rest of them.

Papa hung up the receiver and said they should pray and thank God for deliverance. Of course Papa would say that.

All through the long war months, whenever Papa heard the phrase "The war to end all wars," he would shake his head. "Such nonsense. As long as there are people, there will be wars," he'd say.

By dawn, factory whistles were blowing, church bells were pealing, and people were running everywhere. Uncle Erik called the Schmidt family again to let them know there was to be a parade down Washington Avenue and all businesses were declaring a holiday.

The city was in a fever-pitch of activity as Carl grabbed his bundle of papers that morning. Three-inch-high headlines screamed out the victory for the Allies. The boys would sell all their papers on the street corners that day.

The armistice was signed on the eleventh hour of the eleventh day of the eleventh month of 1918. A day Carl would never forget.

The parade wasn't really a parade. Instead the entire city flooded into the streets. People were crying and laughing and dancing and kissing and hugging and cheering all at the same time. Bands blared and automobile horns honked. Many folks brought their own noisemakers, banging pots and pans with soup ladles. The noise was deafening, but no one wanted it to stop. Never had there been anything quite like it.

Carl ran into a laughing, shouting Weldon Pritchard. Carl jumped up on Weldon's back and he rode piggyback down Washington Avenue as the two of them laughed themselves hoarse. "It's over! It's over! The war's over!"

By evening, the mood was somewhat more subdued. City officials had gathered on a makeshift podium, and gallant speeches were given, lauding all the townsfolk for their help with the war efforts.

As dusk drew its dim veil over the city, the street lamps suddenly came on. A hush went over the crowd. Everyone stared at the wonderful lights. They'd not seen the street lamps for months. The lamps had remained unlit in order to conserve fuel—another one of the ongoing war efforts. Tonight, on Armistice Day, light had at last returned to their city.

Tired and weary, Carl rejoined his family, and they began to walk through the dimming light toward home. When they were halfway back to the house, Carl suddenly thought of something, and all his weariness fled.

"Papa, I have something I must go and do. I'll be home directly."

"But Carl, it's getting late. Where are you going?"

"To see a girl named Jillian Oliver."

Tim elbowed Lydia. "I knew it had to be a girl," he said grinning.

"Tomorrow, Son," Mama said. "Tomorrow you may go."

"No, Mama. I've waited a very long time, and I don't want to waste another moment. Finally I won't have to sneak around to see her."

Papa patted his shoulder. "It is a very special day, my son. You go!"

Spinning around, Carl raced toward the trolley stop as fast as his long legs would carry him. More than one war had come to an end.

There's More!

The American Adventure continues with *The Flu Epidemic*. The flu has changed Larry and Gloria Allerton's lives. School has been cancelled. They hardly see their father anymore because he's a doctor. And they can't play with many of their friends because their friends' families have the flu.

Larry's father tells him not to go to the train station to see any of the returning soldiers because he might catch the flu from them. One day, Larry sneaks off to the train station anyway. A few days later, the entire family has the flu. Larry and Gloria recover, but their mother and younger brother are deathly ill. Larry wonders, *Will my mother and brother die because I disobeyed?*